The Hutenghast

by

GP Matthews

Copyright © 2023 GP Matthews

ISBN: 9781916696419

All rights reserved, including the right to reproduce this book, or portions thereof in any form. No part of this text may be reproduced, transmitted, downloaded, decompiled, reverse engineered, or stored, in any form or introduced into any information storage and retrieval system, in any form or by any means, whether electronic or mechanical without the express written permission of the author.

This is a work of fiction. Names and characters are the product of the author's imagination and any resemblance to actual persons, living or dead, is entirely coincidental.

The views expressed in this work are solely those of the author and do not necessarily reflect the views of the publisher, and the publisher hereby disclaims any responsibility for them.

The Telling

From faded fable and old folklore
From whispered words and thoughts no more
The fear of death from whence he came
The Hutenghast it is his name
He can sense your moisture and see your soul
Wherever you are there's no control
He knows too much to let you go.

He's from the mountains and the wood
He's always near whether you're bad or good
And while you sleep he'll find a crack
Creep into your dreams, there's no way back
Whether newly born or bent and old
The Hutenghast will seek your soul
He knows what makes you tick.

You can hide in a fortress, or build an ark
Turn off the lights and in the dark
He'll creep along like a willowy ghost
And suck the moisture from your throat
He'll whisper gently in your ear
There's no escape, and in your fear
The life is drained from you.

Cunning like fox and strength of bear
With slavering snout and matted hair
Extended arms and steel like grip
Scratch and scrape and chip chip chip
The Hutenghast can smell your soul

Invading your dreams his endless goal
His only focus is your demise
He sees the moisture in your eyes
He'll never let you live.

Both the jaded of heart and the shining brightly
The Hutenghast prowls for you nightly
You may pray or cower in your bed
Either way you'll end up dead
Devoid of moisture and like a prune
Your loved ones find you in your doom
Another lost to him.

Most stories end on a note so bright
Past darkened days into the light
But the tale of the Hutenghast is forlorn
There is no redemption or sunny morn
For no God or Devil knows his birth
He's not of the sky or bound by earth
He's of our dreams and this I say
The Hutenghast may pass your way

And if he does no knight will come
No rescuer, for his will be done
No wringing hands or pious thoughts
Can help you now for all is nought
The Hutenghast has come a calling
No point in screaming or cat-a-walling
He's locked on to your very soul
No heavenly or earthly hole
Of refuge is there for you now.

For the Hutenghast has come your way
Your moisture gone, your flesh decay
Off now you go to endless night
All fear is gone, your lifeless flight
The Hutenghast has passed on through
He came for me and now it's you
Watch out! Here he comes.

He sees you in the dead of night
You can't escape though you think you might
As no heavenly body, or earthly form
Can stop him now, your parents mourn
Tomorrow when they think you'll wake
Mother or father will not mistake
Your shrunken form inside your bed
Now endless screams will fill their heads
The Hutenghast has passed your way
Your wasted life's all gone, decay.

But there is a way to avoid this fate
This written word it is the bait
For The Hutenghast to be called to arms
And if he's not, there can be no harm
Only these words spoken bring the dread
Please read them only in your head
For if these words be voiced aloud
All who hear them will be cowed.

The Hutenghast he will not rest
Till the moisture's gone from every breast
Of all who hear and all who know
He'll seek you high or look below

No hiding place whether earth or sky
Will shield you now as by and by
The hunt is on for you!

Stay awake!, or his will be done
As eyelids shut, and dreams they come
The Hutenghast will be on his way
To drain the life from all who lay
Upon their beds in fitful sleep
Into your dreams he will creep
Your moisture is his greatest prize.

These written words they hold the key
Destroy them not, or all will see
That the Hutenghast cannot be sated
Neither all your love nor all your hatred
Can hinder now or stop the end
Of all that you call foe or friend.

So, bury it quickly, or find a nook
Hide it where no one can look
And as your moisture drains away
And your wasted life falls to decay
One solitary crumb of comfort find
The knowledge that no one left behind
Beyond whom heard these words gone past
Need fear the tale of The Hutenghast!

Foreword

The old lady rocked back and forth metronomically in her chair, waiting, waiting, always waiting. She knew that this life cycle was almost done, and the time remaining to her now was so short. Already she could feel the subtle signs of terminal decay. These 'signs' came on her so quickly now, quicker each time in fact (***all will be revealed***). Where once her hair was thick and dark, her skin soft and lustrous, there was now thin dry white straw for hair and almost translucent parchment skin stretched over her pointed cheekbones. Her hands were twisted and thin, and the hack in her voice was the tell-tale sign that she was approaching the point of transition. Transition not from life into death and the hereafter, but the transition from old to new, birth to rebirth. To the unknowing, this sounds like the desperate dreams of an old maid craving to have the opportunity to live her life over, redress the mistakes, travesties and wrongs done to her during her life. To the unknowing she looks like an octogenarian dwelling on the 'what ifs' and 'if onlys'. But the unknowing are also the uneducated, the uninformed, the unprepared. For this old lady has a secret, yes a dark secret. She has been here before, near death had been a bedfellow to her on more than one occasion, it was a friend, it was a saviour, it was a redeemer.

The first time she 'Refreshed' she felt sorry for the ones who had made the ultimate sacrifice for her. She felt guilty, she knew it was wrong, but the lure of the absolute reward outweighed all of her concerns and so she took that fatal step. It felt like a giant leap of faith at the time, but in reality it was just the last desperate attempts of an old woman to cling on to her drab, meaningless and worthless little life. Of course, nobody wants to die, and the old lady was no exception, and so when she was given the choice on that fateful day, she took it, and why not, who wouldn't? She was dying anyway so why not roll the dice, take that chance. It seemed so preposterous, but the old lady had looked and sounded so calm, so genuine, so nice. If she had stopped to think about it for too long she knew for certain that she would have chickened out, which was something she'd been doing that all her life. From every false dawn, through all the missed opportunities to every ultimate dead end. Yes her 90 years on this earth were a glowing testament for the risk averse, the under-achiever, the abject failure. This time she knew that she had had enough of all the mediocrity, and the disappointments. Here she was at the end of her life, she had no husband, no children, no family, abandoned at birth and brought up in a children's home, she didn't even know who she really was, what a waste. All these things flashed through her mind, and she knew what she had to do and so she did it, she did it, and it worked! It was beyond all belief, but it had actually worked. She knew of course that there was a great darkness at play here. She also knew that there would be a reckoning, but she didn't care, not anymore, and why would she? She looked long and hard in the mirror and what she saw was that she was now young and beautiful again. Learning to live with the guilt would be relatively easy for her, after all this was her right, it was her entitlement. She was (at last) a somebody, she had taken that fateful step and it felt wonderful, invigorating, her whole being pulsed with renewed vigour, a renewed life, and things were going to change. She would show the world who she was, and what she could do.

The sad reality of course was that she was in essence still the exact same person she had always been, but now she had a dark secret. She quickly learned as time went on that this was a trap, a spider's web of entrapment, a ghoulish game, and she was just a pawn within it. She realised that from now on her focus was to be always wary. She would have to keep a low profile, distance herself completely from everyone and everything that she had known in her first 90 pitiful years on earth. This sick and twisted thing that she had now signed up to, was her salvation, and also her inevitable destruction all wrapped up in one. If only she had stopped to think longer, been more rational, more measured, less desperate. If she had, she would be dead and gone long ago, so she told herself that this was always the right thing to do, and it was, wasn't it? Anyway, it was too late now to reconsider. The runes were cast, and so she had to go on, and she knew, right there and then, that when the wheel of time came round full circle that she would always have to make this choice again, but that seemed too far off to contemplate, so she put it to the back of her mind and carried on. 'The Telling' (**all will be revealed**), was safely hidden away until it would be needed again and the dance between life and death would renew once more.

Life is so short. The second time of refreshing she found that the guilt was a little easier to live with. Of course, she knew it was still very wrong, but she told herself that she had been deceived. It wasn't her fault, someone else would do it in place of her and get all the benefits that she had enjoyed during this second span of life. The lure of life was stronger now and it has a way of winning every time. Victims became mere casualties, all of which were inevitable as long as none of them were her, that was all that mattered now. BUT when the time came for second renewal she was shocked. She hadn't been told that each cycle would be shorter by ten years, she found this out when at only 79 she was here again, grasping at life from the jaws of death, and then the true enormity of what she had brought on herself really started to sink in.

The third time she began to feel 'vindicated' somehow, she was 69 and the pattern was clearly set, she knew where she was going and what had to be done but more importantly she knew that she could never quit, so she embraced the madness and was consumed by it. Eventually she didn't care at all about 'The Seven' (***all will be revealed***), they were mere vassals, a means to an end, of no consideration or worth, it was only she that mattered now. She was going to see this thing through, it was what she was now, the die that she had cast so long ago had thrown her into this madness, but she was determined to win. Somehow she was going to destroy the hex that it had put upon her, this slow countdown to oblivion. She didn't know what that meant exactly, or even what she wanted anymore out of life. One thing was certain, this was now 'her game' and she played it so well!

As she rocked back and forth in her chair she looked at image in the mirror on the mantle. Her visage was just as it was the first time before the game had begun but there was something about her that was different, she couldn't quite place what it was, but it was like she was looking at an evil twin, it looked like her but different, dark, knowing, dangerous. Even now after all this time she didn't like what she had become, it was as if she were trapped inside a mannequin, a cyborg, a machine that still looked like her but was something other worldly and bad. Yes even now, a little piece of the original self was still inside her, peeping out and then quickly retreating again, unable to bear for more than a few moments the enormity of it all. There was no fight left inside her, but the candle still flicked briefly each time just before the dance would begin all over again. It was like she almost had a chance to.., but no she was too weak, too worthless, the mirror smiled at her as she looked on, and she knew the game was afoot and the dance would soon begin all over again.

A smile spread across the old lady's sunken face giving her a sort of demented look, devoid of any warmth or feeling. Oh, she could now sense that the wheels were turning, and she felt the electricity of it as the excitement fluttered in her chest. The one solitary thing that comforted her as the time drew near was the certain knowledge that the dark forces controlling all the cogs and wheels of her life would move and creak. Life paths would sway and intersect, unknowing forces that she had long ago stopped trying to understand would present her with the necessary 'fuel' to ignite the life force once more. The life force that now ebbed away, exiting her arteries and her veins in a literal metabolic blur. She didn't panic, she had been here before, there was an inner calm in her that was unsettling to that small flicker inside which was now so small, so insignificant, but still there somehow, surviving against all odds, and in spite of all that she had done to try to extinguish it. She was calm. For she knew that the provision was coming, it was inevitable, unstoppable and she was ready once again, to play the game of The Hutenghast!

Part I

Chapter 1

The alarm gradually invaded the fog and Colin Hart opened his eyes blinking rapidly. The sun so rudely thrusting him into a new day, as he realised that he had forgotten to shut the curtains when he went to bed the night before. The spring sunshine now streamed directly through his bedroom window and across his face.

'Curtains!' he said to himself as he extinguished the noise of the clock with his clenched fist, and then drew his forearm across his face shielding it from the unwelcome light. He wanted to sleep a little longer, but the night's spell was broken, and so he just lay there listening to all the auditory stimulation that gradually pushed sleep further and further away. The stairs creaked, he knew his mother was on her way downstairs to make breakfast, and get his lunch ready for school. At the all-knowing age of twelve, Colin already knew that school was a total drag, and practically a complete waste of time, but it did give him something to do to break up the monotony of waiting to grow up so he could leave and go on an adventure, alone, or with his mates. He didn't mind which mates, as long as he got away from here to somewhere completely different and to do something utterly exciting, somehow.

Colin was twelve years old, blue eyed, auburn haired and freckled of face, as is often the case with fair skinned and auburn-haired children. He was a little overweight, which bothered him, but not enough to really curb his healthy appetite. He was quiet on the whole, a deep thinker, and fiercely loyal to his friends.

Colin had always had the feeling that he was destined for something big one day, but he had long ago decided it was prudent to keep all that stuff to himself for now rather than to be told, 'Oh that's nice dear,' by his mum, who would probably use the same sentence even if he had told her that there was a large spider on her head! If he told his mates, they would most likely just punch him in the arm and say 'Don't be a complete divet Col.'

Mrs Hart was not a good listener; grown-ups never really are. Are they? Sure, they sort of listen on the surface to what their kids have to say to them, but they never really take any of it in. What do kids know about the world, just humour them. The irony of this little fact, and the fact that he didn't really listen to what his mother had to say either, was not as lost on Colin as you may expect. He was a perpetual under achiever in class, but he was in actual fact, a pretty smart kid (whether Mrs Hart actually realised this is or not, is not really relevant to this particular story so we will park it there for another time).

Mrs Hart, (despite her inability to listen to Colin as she scurried through her chores), was an attentive mother, and the aroma of this attentiveness reached Colin's nose just about the same time as she uttered those same familiar eighteen words that she uttered every weekday morning in school term time. That utterance being, 'It is eight o'clock! breakfast is on the table Colin, hurry up or it will get cold.'

Most kids Colin knew (in fact all the kids he had ever asked) ate a cereal-based breakfast practically every day, but Mrs Hart always sent her husband and her son off to work, and to school, with something warm. 'To line their tummies for the day,' as she said. Neither of them ever complained, it was their mutual and silently agreed little 'rite of passage' to eat a cooked breakfast on a cold winter's morning, as well as struggling through a steaming bowl of porridge on a baking summers day, when it was 30 degrees in the shade outside. 'Take the good with the bad son, anything is better than grapefruit and yoghurt,' was what his dad always said, and Colin agreed with him whole heartedly.

Bizarrely Colin missed his dad more at breakfast time than probably any other time of the day. They would sort of smile and wink at each other each morning as they ate that particular hot repast in silence.

For the record, Colin's dad is not dead. He is just in hospital and has been there for about six months following what his mum said was an 'aneurysm'. Colin wasn't really sure what that was at the time, but he knew that he didn't like the sound of it, so he just said 'Oh OK.' Then immediately went upstairs to look it up on his mobile.

Later that same day, his mum had been more forthcoming about his father's condition. She had said 'Well dear, basically your dads in a coma. So, we just have to get on with it ourselves until he wakes up, don't we?' And that was it! Stoicism was always one of her strong suits, but being the smart kid that he was, Colin knew that really she felt just like a tiny sail lost and alone in a stormy sea that was facing a strong wind, and desperately trying to just keep everything afloat. Colin also knew that he had to help and support his mum without being too obvious about it, because that would just make her panic. He was giving it his best try to keep the family ship afloat all on his own, in his enclosed twelve-year-old way until the skipper came back home again.

Today's breakfast was not steaming hot porridge today though, it was, in fact bacon and eggs, Colin's well-tuned nose could tell that even from his bedroom, and it was his particular morning favourite, usually only reserved for weekends, or on the first or last day of each school term too, with no exceptions. That was when reality dawned, this was also a no exception day. He remembered that today was actually the first day back to school after the Easter hols. (it was almost worth it for the breakfast, but not quite).

Reluctantly, he got up, put on his slippers and dressing gown, turned the tap on and off in the bathroom (so his mum would think that he had washed his hands and face), and then he wandered downstairs to digest his favourite breakfast. As he put the pepper and salt on his eggs Colin was totally unaware that the dark forces that control the wheels and cogs of all our lives were turning and moving and slowly but surely, they were pointing in his direction.

Far away an old lady grimaced and cackled as all the players were being chosen by some unseen force and Colin was indeed being lined up along with all the others to play the game of The Hutenghast.

Chapter 2

As Colin ate his breakfast he could not possibly foresee what was about to happen. Nobody can predict the future can they? Except maybe a certain old woman, who was so very secure in her knowledge that she knew the future, for herself and also 'the chosen seven.' Soon, soon, she thought, as she waited, waited.

It is a known fact that boys are not the most astute of people when it comes to things outside of their own 'private little universes,' and they are also not the deepest of thinkers, especially at twelve years of age. Colin was no different to any of his peers in that regard.

Something did feel a little 'off' today though, a little 'odd' you might say. That morning as he dressed for school he could feel it, but he pushed it to the back of his mind. He decided to concentrate on his primary objectives for the day. Those objectives were namely seeing all his mates, Richard (Rich) Jenkins, Barry (Baz) Gold and Stephanie (Steph) Pritchard to be precise. Particularly 'Rich' and 'Steph', (Rich was his best mate) and as for Steph, well she was also just one of his mates of course, but not quite the same as all the rest (not to him anyway). Colin and Steph had been firm friends since they had met on the first day at infant school. Colin's mind went back to that day often, he clearly remembered them holding hands in the corner of the playground in a totally natural way. A kind of mutual comfort blanket for each other in a big new world, and that first day had cemented a special connection between them that would last a lifetime (so Colin thought). It was special to them, they were connected somehow, always together, joined at the hip you might say, a united front against the world.

It seemed like this was always going to be the case, but as they grew up other 'friends' came into their little bubble, and ever so slowly, over time, things changed. First it was Steph's 'girlfriends.' She spent more and more separate time with them, and they spoke about things that Colin wasn't really interested in. Of course, Colin did the same with the boys too, but he couldn't make that connection in his head (typical, I hear all the girls reading this say).

One day Colin overheard a conversation between Steph and the other girls which led him to believe that she had a particular soft spot for Rich. At the time he felt a little 'odd' about the whole thing, but he wasn't quite sure how he should handle it either, and so of course he never mentioned it to any of his friends. Colin was not one to make any unnecessary scene, or to draw any attention to himself. Most of the kids and teachers didn't even know that his dad was in hospital. He kept his feelings to himself, easier to handle, less complicated too. He did however begin to feel a little jealous about this shift in the dynamic, after all Rich was so popular, so sporty, such good fun, in fact he was 'the best' at everything really, so why wouldn't Steph, or any of the other girls for that matter, fancy him. Colin himself on the other hand was a different proposition, he knew he was a little overweight and had recently developed a stammer when put under pressure in class. This was something his enemies at school had begun to take great delight in, which of course just made everything worse. 'Nobody would ever fancy me,' he thought. 'Why would they? Friendship is enough, so don't lose that too by acting like a nerd,' he had said to himself.

Overriding all of these little social and personal issues that seemed to occupy Colin's mind most of the time these days was the cast iron belief that thick or thin you have to stand by your mates whatever happens, and now that his home life was 'more complicated' this seemed to be even more important to him than ever before.

If Steph and Rich were going to be an item, he figured that he could live with that, as long as the bond between them all was never broken, because if it was then he knew that he would be truly lost. His friends were his tether, his rock, and nothing was going to get in the way of that, ever!

Chapter 3

Stephanie Pritchard was awake extra early. It was Monday morning, the first day of a new term, and she hadn't seen her friends at all since last term had ended. She had been away with her parents for the holidays on a cruise through the Norwegian Fjords. It had all been great for them, but not quite so enthralling for her. It was quite exciting when the wind blew, and the waves got up though. She recalled that she had wanted to stand at the bow of the ship, just like Kate Winslet, but that was not possible because 'it was too rough to go out.' So, she had to amuse herself in other ways, which was kind of difficult when she was the only person even remotely 'young' on-board. OK, it was fun dressing up for dinner and stuff, but she had been more than happy when it was time to disembark, come home, and get back to normality.

Steph had that perfect combination, she was pretty, intelligent and smart, which made her universally popular. She liked school, enjoyed learning and was a very bright student too, but most of all she liked the friendship, and the camaraderie that she had with her school friends. These friends were Briony (BB) Brown, who she was closest to, Veronica Harmon (V), Rachel Styles (or Rach).

When it came to boys she wasn't that bothered really, but she did have a secret 'thing' for Richard Jenkins. He was so 'unfazed' by everything. He wasn't very studious, but he was quick witted and good at sports. He just enjoyed himself. He was annoying in lots of ways, but you just couldn't help but like him. Sometimes at school she would suddenly catch herself looking across at him in class, and then look away quickly cursing herself a little as she did so. She didn't know why really. Rich seemed oblivious to her as anything special, she was just one of the gang to him, but she noticed that he did seem to have taken a particular interest in Briony, which was also very annoying. Again, she didn't really know why. Lastly there was Colin. She had known him, like forever. He was reliable and thoughtful and everything a friend should be, but well, when you've heard absolutely everything each other has to possibly say about stuff, then what is there left to talk about? Sure, he was still in her circle of friends, but he had dropped off her 'interest scale' a little as she had gotten older.

Steph combed her hair, and she daydreamed a little as she looked at her reflection in the mirror. Out of nowhere she felt a sudden chill, goosebumps appeared on her arm, just like when someone is walking over your grave (as her nan always said). It was really odd, because she was only thinking about nice things. The trip that they were all going on was coming up soon. It was a field trip, hiking in the Bavarian Alps, all very exciting.

She had no idea whatsoever of course that at the precise moment that the chill happened, it was a portent of things to come, and the Bavarian trip was to be the catalyst to put into motion all the cogs and wheels that the dark forces in this world control.

Steph ate her breakfast, got dressed and hopped into the car. Her mum took her the three miles to school just as she always did, (the only time her dad took her to school was when he had time off work, or had to work from home as there was a train strike and he couldn't get into the city). Steph's dad was something in finance, she didn't really know what, but she had nice clothes, a pony and she was loved, so she was happy. She would be happier still when she saw her friends though. Two weeks without proper girl gossip was an eternity at the age of twelve, mobile phones are great but reception was mixed and 'too expensive' in Norway, so basically she had had zero contact with her friends, and she was aching to see Rich too, but that was her secret, nobody knew she had a 'thing' for him, they couldn't possibly. Her mates definitely didn't have a clue, that was for sure. Once girls know you fancy a boy, then it's pretty relentless (their excitement and goading and all that). Steph didn't want that complication or pressure just yet. Sure, she liked Rich, but 'the gang' was always paramount. Us against the rest (the rest being primarily Keith Henderson and the Duke twins). Every school has bad apples, and these three were rotten to the core. They were rude to the girls, rough with the boys (when they outnumbered them of course, as all classic bullies are basically cowards). She hated the way they made fun of Colin's stammer too, something burned hot inside her when they made fun of him, and belittled him in class. She was the only one of the girls who knew that his dad was in hospital, she assumed that Rich knew too, as he was Colin's best friend, but they never spoke about it, and Colin never used it as an excuse to get sympathy either (he probably realised that would fall on deaf ears anyway with those three). So, he never said a word, and she felt the pain for him. Mates 'the gang' were everything to her, even reliable old Colin.

Chapter 4

Meeting up in the playground before the bell sounded at 9am was such a routine thing, but it always came with an extra tinge of anticipation and excitement on the first day of term. Catching up and looking forward was always that little bit keener on the first day back.

Colin walked through the school gate and into the yard. He was normally one of the first ones in the playground each morning, but since his dad had been in hospital, the metronome that was Mrs Hart, was a little more erratic, and this particular day he got to school at 8:59 am. Colin scanned the crowd, and saw his mates over on the far side by the bike sheds. They were all there, Steph, Rich (stood next to each other), and also Barry Gold, plus the girls too.

'About time you got here Cart Horse,' said Keith Henderson (the school bully), as he laid eyes on Colin. The Duke twins (Peter and Brian) laughed like two idiots are inclined to do, but Colin as usual just ignored them and went straight over to his friends.

'Hi,' he said.

'Don't listen to those morons Col,' said Rich. 'They are not worth it, a waste of oxygen mate. How are things?'

'Er, yeah, Ok thanks,' said Colin.

Then the bell saved him, and into school they all walked.

School was a series of generic drab buildings, typical of schools that had been built around the country during the late 50's and early 60's. There was a tower block for the form rooms, and several separate one- and two-story buildings for science, crafts and sports facilities etc. There was an expanse of playing fields to the rear, and to the side were hardcourts for tennis, netball and five a side etc. It could have been any average school in any unremarkable town, and on the face of it, it was, but the wheels and cogs were turning, dark forces were stirring, and the icy finger of evil was pointing in their direction. Not the whole school of course, just at seven souls, seven souls out of the many countless souls in the world that could have been ear-marked for the dark game of The Hutenghast. Seven souls, preferably innocent and unsullied but always oblivious, and most important of all, pulsating with life and ready to be plucked.

That subject aside, the air this morning was thick with the hum of chatter and laughter as everyone separated off once inside the reception area, and walked off towards their respective form rooms. Col, Steph, Rich, Baz, BB, V, and Rach, were all in the same form, and so they all headed off in the same direction. Up two flights of stairs in the tower block, and through the door into form room 4C. Keith Henderson and the Duke twins (who were also in the same form as the gang) had sloped along a few paces behind them, sneering and sniggering, as they always did, even though nobody paid any attention to them.

The room was laid out pretty much the same as any you would expect to see in any generic classroom. There were several rows of desks for the children, and just inside the door there was a larger, taller desk, directly in front of a large white board, which had various smudged scribblings still evident on it from the last lesson of the previous term.

Sat at this large desk was their form teacher, Mr Ford. He was a fairly stout, barrel-chested man that somewhat resembled an Army Sergeant Major, although he was no military man. He was in his mid-thirties, and had thin sandy hair which was receding rather too rapidly for his liking.

The girls didn't care for him that much. They all found him a bit overbearing, but the boys thought he was OK 'for a teacher.' After all he liked sports, which was always a good thing for conversation, and he drove a sports car too (the girls thought the car made him look a little desperate and sniggered when they saw him driving past in it with his thin hair flapping in the breeze), but the boys thought it was cool.

The girls also knew that he was having 'a relationship' (of sorts) with Miss Rhymer who was their English teacher. The boys, of course, were completely oblivious to this unimportant piece of information, and so it was never discussed between the sexes.

It is a known fact that girls develop much more quickly than boys do, and at twelve years of age they are highly tuned to pick up on every signal regarding relationships, not just within their own age group but amongst the teachers too. As for the boys, they were still children in that regard, according to them. Largely this is true of course, but Colin was a very sensitive boy, and he picked up on many of the same things that the girls did, but rather than 'blab' about it, as they were prone to do. As was his way, he kept his own council on such matters.

Mr Ford waited a minute or so for the hubbub to subside, and when it was clear that was not going to quieten, he tapped his ruler on the desk.

'OK, OK, settle down now, take your seats, and let's get this term started shall we ladies and gents?' he said. 'Plenty of time to chin wag during break or lunch. This is school time now, expand your minds time.'

A voice at the back whispered, 'And your waistline Sir.'

'What was that Henderson?' said Mr Ford.

'Nothing, Sir, just agreeing with you,' said Henderson.

OK, well, register call then.'

Mr Ford went through all the names. He called them out one by one, waiting for the response 'here' before he moved on to the next.

'A full complement,' he said. 'Very good, off you go now to your classes. Oh, I nearly forgot. All those of you that are going on the school trip to Bavaria in two weeks' time, I will need your parents to pay the balance by this Friday at the very latest, clear? So that means you Hart and you too Gold.'

'They probably can't afford to go Sir,' said Henderson.

'Quiet boy!' said Mr Ford, as the Duke twins sniggered. He turned to Colin and Barry and said in a quieter tone, 'Don't forget boys, by this Friday please.'

'Yes Sir,' they said in unison as they all filed out the door and off to maths, which was the first lesson on the day.

At lunch break the gang assembled in the playground as was the norm for them.

'So, are you two going on the trip then?' said BB. 'You are leaving it a bit late after all.'

'I told my mum to hold off until she has to pay, otherwise she loses interest at the bank,' said Baz. (Barry was a very astute person for his age). 'I will bring a cheque in Friday morning, and then everyone will be happy, including me of course. This is going to be great.'

'Yes me too' said Rich. 'I have never been abroad before, so the whole thing will be an absolute blast, right Col?'

'Er, yeah, I guess it will,' said Colin deep in thought.

'You are still coming though, right?' said Steph.

'Yeah of course, my mum's a bit.. er.. forgetful at the moment that's all, I will remind her when I get home,' said Colin.

The subject was dropped and thought no more of, and they gradually separated out into boy and girl groups to talk about more pressing matters like football, or fashion and make up.

By the end of the school day everybody had caught up with everyone else. They knew precisely what all the others had or hadn't done over the Easter holidays. It seemed that apart from them all eating a little too much chocolate, only Steph had done anything vaguely exciting, (of course she omitted to tell her friends that the Norwegian cruise thing was actually all a bit of a bore). 'Yes, it was great,' she said. 'Lots to do, all the dressing up for dinner etc.' And so on.

Colin looked at her, smiled and thought 'Yes, great this, fab that, who are you kidding me, that's for sure.'

Steph glanced at him, and reddened a little. She could immediately tell that he knew the truth, and that was OK, because she also knew for certain, that he would never say anything to the others.

The week flew by, and things got back to normal as they always tend to do, Colin thought as he was walking home after school on that Thursday afternoon.

'Well Steph still secretly likes Rich, who still seems far more interested in annoying BB.' Being a clever lad, he knew that meant he liked her, and he was glad, because if Rich liked Steph as much as she seemed to like him then, well he thought that he wouldn't care for that too much. Making fun of your friends in a nice way was a good thing of course, all part of building friendships, it was only when it was horrible like Henderson saying nasty things about everyone, taking the opportunity to bully when he had the Dukes in tow but sneering from a distance when they were not around. That was not so good. The rest of the gang didn't know why he was so horrible to everyone, but

Colin figured there was a reason, he used to be OK! Whatever it was, he just tried to keep away from him and say nothing.

Then there was Barry, good old Baz. Clever, always dependable, and a good mate. The other girls V and Rach were always together, they lived three doors away from each other and their parents had always been friends. That meant that they got to see each other at evenings and weekends too, so they had a different bond than the rest of the gang in a way, but were still of course an integral part of it.

Colin was glad to be back at school with his mates. It was like a haven, especially as things seemed so uncertain at home, but he knew that he had to just plough on until things changed.

He got to the garden gate and saw his mum in the garden taking in some clothes from the line.

'Hello dear,' she said. 'I've put a cheque on your bed for the school trip, so don't forget to take it in tomorrow, the letter said it had to be paid by then.'

Colin smiled and thought 'Baz would be impressed.' 'Thanks Mum,' he said as he went in and up to his room.

Chapter 5

The old lady was patient, she knew that all things were in hand, and that comforted her. As she sat there, her mind wandered, as it often did, to the fateful day all those years ago when she was in her first life and nearing the end. She had received a strange letter asking her to travel to Bavaria to meet with someone she had never met. All she knew was that the letter was signed Emily. The old woman had led a quiet uneventful life, and was not prone to flights of fancy or adventure, but the letter was so intoxicating, not really telling her why to come, or what this was all about. There was nothing there that any sane person would take any notice of, and yet, between the words, there was something intangible. It was madness, but she knew that she had to go, and so on the allotted day, at the given time, she travelled to that small village in Bavaria to visit this Emily. All the expenses had been taken care of, both ways. All she had to do was go and listen, and then come home. She was eighty-nine years of age, and so this was quite an undertaking for her to travel all the way to Bavaria from her little cottage in the heart of The Cotswolds. 'One adventure before I die,' she thought. That thought tingled with excitement inside her chest, but was also equally heavy on her heart, as she pondered over all her wasted years. She had such a short time left to her now, and so she decided to meet whatever lay ahead, head on and with a positive mind.

As she alighted at the station, she scanned around looking for the taxicab that the letter told her would be waiting. She felt a presence at her side and looked around to see a man standing there. He was neatly dressed in a dark suit. He picked up her bag. He had such a blank face, 'Unremarkably plain,' she thought. She was just about to speak when he said, 'This way ma'am the lady is expecting you.'

Without waiting for a reply, he walked off with her bag in his hand towards a large black cab. It was sort of a cross between a taxi and a hearse, 'too large for one job, too small for the other,' she thought as she followed him.

It wasn't long before she found that the driver was not one for small talk or indeed talking at all, because he failed to answer either of the only two questions that she had put to him practically as soon as she had sat down in the cab.

'Where are we going exactly?' and 'Is it very far?' she had asked, but he just kept driving and so she thought, oh well maybe his English is not good, or he's just not very gregarious, (which she wasn't herself), and so she let it go, and settled back in the leather seat. They drove onwards towards who knows where, for a reason that was still a complete mystery to her.

Emily sat and peered out of the window waiting for her guest to arrive. Her feelings were mixed, she had refreshed for the very last time only recently, and the descent from youth to old age was swift but tapered. The first six months she had looked in the mirror each morning, and she saw no change to her appearance. Her looks, her vigour, were all intact, unchanged, but she knew from all the past refreshing's, that as time got nearer her body would start to wither and fail. She knew this was her last life cycle and she had so wanted to enjoy these ten years as much as she could, but all the time it had just felt like a clock was ticking, a gun was at her temple, the sands of time were rushing through the glass, and each morning she awoke expecting to see a change, a shift towards demise. But this time it was different, nothing had changed. One year became two, three, five, six and she still felt as good as ever she had. She still looked just as beautiful, why was this so?

She dared to believe that the spell was broken after all this time, after all she had fulfilled her side of the arrangement right to the end. Maybe her reward was to have one last normal life and not wither and die within ten years as she had expected, she had certainly earned it she told herself. All those souls taken to save her own, and to also to fortify the beast.

She tried not to think of the beast. She had been relatively unaware of his existence that first time, but for every up there is a down, and she found out very quickly as her time approached at the end of that first refreshing that the life force of the seven was primarily to fortify this beast, her assistance was required merely as a lure, and her reward was a small portion of that life force stolen from the innocent to maintain the beast's existence.

Her life extensions were merely a by-product. She was a vassal, a means to an end, but she still dared to dream of one last normal life.

On the first day of the tenth year after her last refreshing she awoke and got out of bed. She felt cold, even though the sun shone brightly outside. She went across the room to her side table as she did every day, she picked up her silver hand mirror, and gazed into it. What she saw made her drop the mirror and scream, she picked it up again and looked hard. The image before her was still her, but overnight she had gone from youth to.. well, something horrendous. What she saw were deep lines appearing on her face, her teeth were yellowing, and her hair was streaked with grey. Her hands were bony, and the skin was beginning to wrinkle. 'No, no, no!' she cried. But it was a weary cry for secretly she had known that nothing good would ever come to her again. She turned, sat at her desk, opened the drawer, drew out paper and pen, and started to write a letter.

The letter that she wrote to the old lady Margaret that day, was much as the one she had received herself all those many years ago. All the details of who to contact, then when's and what to write etc. had all come to her in vivid dreams, so vivid in fact, that each and every detail became etched into her mind, impossible to forget, impossible to get wrong. She prepared as her predecessor must have done all those years ago. The two parchments were taken from their resting place ready for the next great cycle for The Hutenghast, for which Emily had played her part, She was now fulfilling her final role before the peace that was promised to her in the first parchment would come (she often wondered if this were true or was it just more deception and lies), she was far too deep and way too distant from what she once was, to do anything other than to merely obey. It was time for her to hand the baton over to Margaret and diminish.

Margaret was daydreaming and drifting in and out of sleep when the taxi came to an abrupt halt, and she came to with a jolt. 'Are we here?' she asked the driver, who remained stubbornly mute. He opened the door, extending his arm in a 'this way' gesture towards the large house that was before them. It had a gothic look about it but was adorned with flower beds and hanging baskets that softened the austere look to a large degree.

She got out of the taxi, took her bag and walked towards the front door which seemed to almost open by itself. She hesitated for a moment, then continued as the door swung wider, and an elderly lady came into view. She stared at her as if looking into a mirror, as they were so alike that they could have been siblings, twins even. She remembered her manners and turned to thank the driver, but the taxi was no longer there (later she recalled that there were no tyre tracks to be seen on the gravel driveway to show that any vehicle had even been there) but at that moment her host spoke, and she thought of it no more.

'Good afternoon my dear,' said her doppelganger.

'Are you Emily?' she said.

'I am indeed, and welcome Margaret, thank you so much for coming. I so hoped that you would. Come in, I have tea waiting in the library.'

Margaret followed her through the entrance hall with its large staircase. It was rather reminiscent of the hall in Gone With The Wind's Tara. They walked through a door on the right side beneath the staircase which opened into a large room filled with shelves of books on three sides, the fourth wall was open, save for a large fireplace and mantle with flowers and paintings above. In front of the fireplace was a small round table and two chairs and on the table was a silver tea service and cups, and an assortment of cakes.

'Please take a seat,' Emily said and the old lady dutifully obliged.

As she opened her mouth to speak the old lady was interrupted by Emily.

'Tea, milk, sugar?'

'Oh, thank you, just milk please,' she said.

'You must have questions, which is quite understandable my dear, but I can assure you that all the answers are here, and you will be so pleased you came I am sure. But first let us take tea, and you can relax a little after your long trip. Cake?'

'Thank you, no,' said Margaret as she took her teacup and looked around the room. It was quite beautiful, the flowers were lovely, the tea was really good, the books were all beautifully bound in leather and gold, a large clock metronomically ticked beside the staircase to the balcony where even more books sat on even more shelves.

'You have quite an extensive library,' she said.

Emily smiled. 'Yes, I suppose I do, I have been collecting them for many, many years. Please relax and enjoy your tea, we have all the time in the world to discuss why you are here.'

As she was a polite person, never pushy, Margaret allowed the conversation to stop there, and she drank her tea in silence as Emily smiled and sipped her own tea.

When they had finished and after a few polite minutes Margaret opened her mouth to speak when Emily said, 'OK, to the heart of the matter then my dear. Can I ask you a question?'

'Yes, of course,' said Margaret, taken aback a little.

'Do you have regrets, my dear? Life regrets that is. Would you go back and redo things at all?' Emily asked.

Taken aback a little Margaret replied, 'I suppose we would all do some things differently with hindsight, but there is nothing we can do about that.'

'Ah, hindsight, yes,' said Emily. 'Rather cruel in a way don't you think?'

'In a way I suppose,' said Margaret. 'But you can't change the past can you?'

'How true,' said Emily 'But the future, what about that, Margaret?'

'Yes,' said Margaret 'I think my future is rather short, too late for any big changes for me I think, and also for you if you don't mind me saying,' she said. 'We must be a similar age, I assume.'

'Eighty-nine?' said Emily

'Yes that is correct,' Margaret said thinking that this is all starting to get a little weird. She started to feel uncomfortable. 'I am thankful for your invitation and everything, but could you explain exactly why you asked me to come?'

'What would you say if I told you that your future can be certain, and that you can change many things about your life. Redress any regrets and missed opportunities that you may have had, and make everything perfect?' said Emily.

'What would I say? I would say that what is done is done, and we all have to accept now is our mortality?'

'Margaret, I have a great secret and a great gift to offer you. I am not exactly as you see me, a woman of the same age as yourself, that has lived my life as you have and now I near the end. It is true, I near the end, but I have lived a long, long time. 'You see that book?' She pointed to a large open book on a side table.

'Yes,' said Margaret.

'I purchased that book from a shop in Vienna in 1792. All these books I have purchased over many, many years. Too many for the average person to contemplate Margaret, but neither I nor you are average people. I was chosen, and you have been chosen also to inherit a gift. The gift of life, Margaret.' Emily beamed and even though she was old there was a radiance that Margaret found irresistible.

'I think I've wasted my time coming,' said Margaret as she stood to go. 'I thank you for the tea, can you ask the driver to pick me up and take me back to the station, I can make my own way home from there.'

'Home, yes, do you like your home Margaret?' said Emily, ignoring the request to leave. 'I will come straight to the point,' she said. 'I can offer you my gift of long-life Margaret, I have lived so long, done everything I ever wanted to do and now it is my time to pass this gift to you Margaret. There is nobody else, just you and me. I want you to have what I had, a great gift for which there is no fee, no recourse. Wouldn't you like to live Margaret?, I think you would. I know you would. Look at the book Margaret, there are two parchments on it, one is wrapped in a white ribbon, the other black. They are the secret Margaret. I purchased these from a vendor here in Bavaria a long time ago when I was a young woman,' she lied. 'I was told to put these parchments somewhere very safe and live my life normally. My only instruction was to open the parchment with the white ribbon when I approached my ninetieth birthday and follow the instructions, which I did. I then became twenty-one again and lived another lifespan until it was time to follow the instructions within the parchment once more. I have lived a life so full Margaret; I want that for you. We are kin Margaret, our family tree is intertwined, all I want now is for you to benefit from everything that I have had. Are you brave enough, strong enough, wise enough Margaret? There is no need to be afraid, look at me, my accomplishments, I have seen kings and queens come and go, wars rage and die. My life a constant blessing, now it is your turn Margaret, I give this to you.'

Margaret was dumbstruck, she couldn't think straight, she knew it was crazy but there was something so strong in the words and the expression on Emily's face. It was like she knew her; she was her; they were one. Before she could utter a word, Emily was standing in front of her with the one parchment in each hand.

'Hold these sacred transcripts as I do Margaret and repeat after me the words I speak and all will be yours,' said Emily

Margaret wanted to stop, to think, to run. She desperately wanted to leave, but she stayed. Without thinking her hands opened and her arms lifted, they stretched them out in front of her all by themselves. Then Emily spoke: -

'Hutenghast my time has come
Release this gift
Your will be done.
The times of life
Are circles drawn
An endless line
Never redrawn.
Boundless gifts
Bestowed to me
I now accept
This destiny.'

Even as Emily spoke the words also came out of Margaret's mouth in unison and she felt the parchments in her hands.

As soon as she had spoken the last word a rushing sound pounded her ears. She felt faint but also strong, there was a bright light followed by an unbelievable darkness, so dark that it felt like no light was left anywhere in the universe. Then she opened her eyes and saw a pile of ash where Emily had once stood. She should have felt sick, horrified, scared, but she was calm as a mill pond. She put the parchments in her bag, retraced her steps to the front door and exited. The driver was waiting. 'You can leave now; all is as it should be,' said Margaret. 'This is my new home. When the time comes I will call you.'

The driver got into the car and drove away, no tracks could be seen.

Chapter 6

The Hutenghast stirred and all that were still within his thrall felt the weight of it. He was restless, impatient. He was weaker than he had once been and that enraged him, but he was wily and clever. He knew that he had to conserve, regroup, and move ever forward, as that was the means for him to survive.

Once he had been so strong, there seemed no end to his powers, but over the millennia so many supplicants had failed him, fallen by the wayside. So many worlds and great civilisations had crumbled, and slowly ever so slowly, he had edged towards the unthinkable, his own demise. He was now like a stalactite that was hurtling towards its inevitable nemesis.

The Hutenghast had always been there, right from the beginning of things when 'The Great Being' held all that was, together. Back then, all the divine beings swirled in his presence. There was no matter, no substance, just thought. But within this perfection there grew discord. Thoughts tend to move position, and the divine beings started to move in strange directions, at odds with the great purpose, and so in time The Great Being decided to split the divine, some he kept with him, he cherished them, succoured them, nurtured them, supported them, others he cast down.

Light became separated and darkness came upon the fallen. The beast became form and was driven from the light.

At first it was easy, there were so many opportunities, he was free to roam, do whatever he wished, but evil is self-absorbed, it cannot see its own frailty, and so it was that The Great Being studied and watched over the beast as he scuttled in the darkness slowly sealing his own fate. He foresaw all this, and was content.

The beast raged, schemed and cut a swathe through countless time and worlds, but that was long ago. Earth was once a mere spec of sand on his beach, but now it was so very important, the last true beacon, a flickering flame, his only hope of survival.

The time was approaching, seven souls were needed to fortify his ebbing existence. He was desperate, ever watching as this one last cord that held him stretched and stretched. The great power he once had, was now focused purely on his own survival.

He knew The Great Being was watching him from above, he knew that he was smiling, he knew that he was content. He also knew that he was so sure of how things would transpire (and he had been right). All things had come to pass exactly as he had foretold at the time of the creation. The beast and the other evil forces had all been given a choice, accept the way things are to be, or be cast down. They chose unwisely, and he felt alone, like he was the only one left.

The beast burned with the thought of it, but now it was all tapered down to the very primal, it was now survive or die. He chose to survive, he needed to survive, and so, with all his being, he focused on the old lady Margaret who was the one and only hope for him. He realised just how precarious all things were, and for the very first time he felt real fear. Fear was something he cherished, he used it to wield his influence on others, but now the tables were turned inwards, and he was the one dangling above the precipice. It was not a comfort to him, he bellowed in the dark and he trembled.

Margaret Ballinger, for that was her full title, shivered. She was unaware of the extent of the beast's fall. All she knew was that to keep her soul, she had to play the game, play her part, one slip and she would be cast down, lost.

The 'gift' of extended life through 'refreshing' had not been as she had expected, it was a millstone around her neck, she was never free of the burden, and it weighed down on her so. She sometimes wondered if Emily had fared better than she was doing, she had seemed very together but the more she thought about it the more she realised that they were both mere mice on a wheel, running, running, running. Ever running, and getting nowhere. All she had left to her now was to mark her time, perform, pass on the baton and turn to dust as Emily had done.

But not yet, no not yet. She had refreshing's left to her and she was determined to embrace them, and to find a way somehow to rid herself of this great sin. She was old now, the time was approaching, all things were starting to be put in place again, and so she pushed all these thoughts to the back of her mind and concentrated on the task ahead. When she became young again, then she would plan what to do.

She wondered if the beast (known as The Hutenghast in the earthly tongue) could see through her, could tell what she was thinking, it scared her to think that this may be the case, but what other choice did she have.

The Hutenghast could not sense Margaret Ballinger's thoughts, he could not see into her mind, those powers had been lost to him long ago, but The Great Being could see. He knew all things past, all things present and all things that are yet to come, and so he was content.

Chapter 7

The school days went quickly from the excitement of a new term to the dull daily routine as the time passed by. The school trip was all but forgotten as it was way into the future as far as any twelve-year old's timetable was concerned. It was to be during the coming summer holidays, and they had to get through a whole term with exams and all the accompanying stress of which school they would go to next year. Was it to be the local secondary school or the boys and girls' grammar schools in the next town? Whichever way you looked at it, the gang was going to be split and that worried them all to varying degrees.

Baz and Steph (who were the most studious of the group), were probably the least concerned. It was grammar school for them come hell or high water, not passing the 12+ exam was not an option for them.

Rich wasn't too bothered, although he guessed that the sports facilities would be better at grammar and so he was hoping to get in there.

BB was pretty sure that she would pass and go to the grammar, and she assumed that Steph would go too, so she was pretty OK about the whole thing.

V and Rach wanted to be together above all, and both knew that the exams were going to be tough, and they were concerned about one passing and the other not. They had actually discussed 'flunking' on purpose so they could definitely be together whatever happened, but they also wanted to be with Steph and BB too, so they made up their minds to study really hard, and do their very best.

Colin, tried not to think about it too much, he was a deep thinker, which was always his trouble, and he worried about everything, his mum in particular. Would she be OK if he went to school in the next town? Of course, he knew that she wanted him to go to grammar school, but he felt that he should be near home especially because his dad was not there. He guessed some of the gang would pass and some may not, and so the gang would split whatever happened, and that troubled him. The boys and girls' grammar schools were right next to each other, they shared extensive playing fields, so the ones who passed would still see each other at lunch breaks as well as on the bus to and from etc. That made it feel better, but it was still all change, and Colin didn't want any change. He wanted everything to stay just exactly how it was right now (apart from desperately wanting his dad to come home of course).

Apart from V and Rach, the others never discussed their future schools together or anything about their futures really. What career to choose, whether they wanted a family or not? In fact, any of the things that are so important when you are just a little bit older. They all lived in their twelve-year-old bubble, and that is of course how it should be. There were always things outside of their friendships that caused concerns but mostly that was compartmentalised, home stuff at home, friend stuff and school stuff at school. Some of the gang spent time together outside school, weekends and evenings but they were never really 'all together' during this time, and so this made the school trip to Bavaria all the more special, because they were going to be all together for two whole weeks. No parents just the teachers Mr Ford and Miss Rhymer, and they were not what you would call disciplinarians in any way, so the trip was bound to be great fun, and they were all looking forward to it so much, even Henderson and the Duke twins could not dampen their enthusiasm. Anything beyond the summer could wait, they were just wanting to savour this last precious time together before things would inevitably change forever. They would grow up, go to different schools, that was obvious, but the unspoken fear was that they would grow apart, and gradually the gang would be no more.

Far away Margaret smiled and waited. She had very little personal details about 'the seven' apart from who they were, and where they came from. She was glad for that. There was no need to bring unnecessary emotion into this. It was necessity, pure and simple. Just a transaction, and all she wanted to know was that they would come, and that she would know when, not through anything written on the parchment with the white ribbon, that was just a guide. No, it was just 'going to happen' it always did.

Things came to her in her dreams, as the time approached, and she knew that the beast was always preparing, ever vigilant. Destiny would bring them to her at the allotted time, and therefore she had no fear of failure. That was never an option, the ramifications would be unthinkable, but there was always a plan B.

She had found this out several refreshing's previously when war came and the chosen seven did not come as planned, 'he' told her in a dream what would happen, and it did. Souls had to be taken from the nearby villages which was, she thought, rather risky. But the simple folk were too scared and too stupid and so everything transpired without any problems, and so as she always told herself, all will be well (for us anyway). She cackled to herself and thought of it no more that day.

Chapter 8

The constant 'beep beep' was an annoyance but also a sort of comfort to Mr Hart. He wasn't quite sure what had happened to him, or where he was either, but one thing was certain, he knew that he was trapped 'somewhere.' For a long time, he thought that he was in a cave, or maybe a pothole of some kind, (he used to go pot holing when he was a little younger, and slimmer!), but he didn't have a grasp on timescale as he lay there, and so he wasn't really quite sure about anything. He didn't know what day it was, what year it was, and although that should have worried him, it did not. Something subliminal kept him calm and sane those long six months, although he was not really aware of that time frame.

He had flashes of things, but they were mere moments, and then they were gone. Sometimes he could hear voices nearby. They were talking all around him, and he thought they might also be trapped in the cave. He hoped they were all OK.

Mr Hart couldn't recall anything personal at all, like recollection of a family or friends. All that was too blurry, but he did seem to realise that people would care about him and that was also a comfort.

As time went by and progress was slow, the doctors began to be more and more worried about the outcome here, but Mrs Hart and her son need not be informed just yet, there was still time for healing. The scans showed improvement, but the patient was deeply asleep, so deep that they were concerned that his mind would be permanently damaged, altered, or at least affected in many ways that would be evident if he did finally awake. His temperament and mood could be drastically different, he may not recognise anyone, it was all so uncertain but they had all agreed that now was not the time to despair, and so they monitored him, and kept him as stable as they could.

Mrs Hart visited regularly, and sometimes Colin would come too, but he would usually just sit there not really knowing what to say. It was all so difficult for him. He was a good lad, and he had really stepped up to help her at home ever since this had happened, and she was so grateful to him for that, but here in the hospital, he just looked like a lost lamb as he gazed at his father, and it was all she could do to stop herself crying and scooping him up in her arms. She knew that kind of gesture would freak him out, and so she continued to put on the front that she had maintained 'the stiff upper lip' and 'let's get on with it until your dad comes round' sort of thing, but inside, she was close to breaking point.

Mr Hart didn't really remember things, he was a bit like a goldfish who thought 'Oh there's a rock, there's a castle,' every time he swam past. That was a good thing of course, for to be trapped and to know that months had passed by and your family were desperately in need of you, would have been too much to bear, and so he plodded on in his ignorance, occasionally trying to grab at the flashes that came to him, like they were foot holds and ledges that would lead him out of the dark cave and back into the light.

Unbeknown to Mr Hart, the doctors, and his immediate family, he was being 'watched elsewhere also'. The beast roamed the subconscious world, he spoke in dreams and nightmares to the faithful, but also he watched what I could only describe here as 'a person of interest'. This man was the father of one of the seven, and that is why he kept him low. It pleased him to be able to wield this power, however small it may have been compared to what he used to be able to accomplish. It troubled the boy, and that made him more pliable, more vulnerable and therefore easier to take.

If a beast can smile, he did so as he thought of it. Soon now, soon, and just for fun he would extinguish this man even though he would not gain from it himself, his soul would go before The Great Being, but it pleased him that the power that the seven would bring to him was enough to snuff out this person who dwelled only in the subconscious.

Chapter 9

As the date of the school trip to Bavaria grew nearer, Colin was having strange dreams. He had never really been one to recall any dreams he may have had whilst asleep before, because as soon as he awoke, whatever had been running through his mind while he slept, always seemed to disappear in a puff of smoke. The weird thing was, that these latest dreams nearly always involved his dad. He couldn't ever recall dreaming about his parents before, so that was kind of odd, but mostly it was the nature of the dreams that left him feeling a little disconcerted. Apart from the fact that they were so vivid, it was what they were about and how they played out.

The first dream was just about his dad being in a coma (they never used that word at home, he was just sleeping until he got better). Even though he was in a coma, he could still talk, but it was like a strange language. Colin didn't understand it, it was guttural and dark, and sounded like everything was bad. There was no good in what he was saying Colin knew that for sure, even though he couldn't understand a single word. Also, he spoke with his eyes closed but he inclined his head to face Colin as he spoke, so he knew it was directed at him and nobody else because his mum and the doctors were there too, right on the far reaches of his vision, almost like they were hiding because when he tried to see them they vanished. Yes this was definitely just between him and his dad, but the why of it was a complete mystery to him.

As the nights progressed, so did the dreams. The language was still the same, but Colin could hear words here and there that made sense to him somehow, like this was all a warning. Also, his dad was sometimes sitting in a chair, other times he was wide awake, but he was always looking the other way from Colin's gaze when his eyes were open, and that was when he appeared to be talking to somebody else. He seemed to peer into dark corners as he spoke and became very agitated, his face twitched, and spittle came out as he spoke, like it always did when he was angry about something. Colin suspected that his dad was trying to tell death to go away or something like that, but why was this all coming Colin's way too. He had decided to ask his mum if she slept OK, and did she dream at all, stuff like that. He didn't want to tell her what was happening to him, but he thought that if she said something that made him think dad was visiting her too, then they could maybe talk about it.

'Dreams dear?' she said. 'No, I still sleep like a baby, which sounds odd what with your dad not being here and all that, but, well I just close my eyes at night and when I wake it is time to get up, just the same as ever. Why do you ask?'

'No reason Mum, I remember seeing a programme on the telly once where this family who lived miles apart used to talk to each other in their sleep, I thought maybe dad did that to you that was all,' he said.

'No, I wish he could in a way, but if he did, I expect he'd be telling me I don't water the garden enough, or dead head the flowers or something, I can do without that when I'm asleep, I need my rest. Plenty of time to discuss what I've done wrong when he comes home.'

'You haven't done anything wrong Mum,' he said. 'I just miss him that's all.'

'You and me both dear,' she said. Then she quickly turned and walked away with the hint of a tear in her eye.

And so it was that Colin realised that he was alone in this regard, and it made him concentrate even more to try and figure out what all this was about. He even tried talking to his dad as he slept, but it was like when Scrooge saw his younger self, and his family in A Christmas Carol. He could see his dad, but he couldn't interact with him, and so all he could do was watch and listen, and try to learn what was going on. There had to be a reason for all this, but what was it?

Slowly Colin had started to feel that this wasn't about death and his dad at all, it was about him, Colin, and that made the riddle seem a little more sinister.

The Hutenghast liked to taunt the boy's father. 'It is so easy when they are always in my realm,' he thought. When he needed sustenance, then it was just about taking the seven and that was it, of course he could be in peoples' dreams from time to time anyway, but that was just like being scared of the Bogey Man for them, it wasn't real, he couldn't do anything to them without 'The Telling' being uttered, that was the key. Without that, he was nothing more than a spectre in the dark, here for one dream and then gone.

This was a first for him, a chosen one's father unconscious, contactable for all this time, it was a pleasure for him, a very small victory here and there in a great sea of nothing, was a real gift, and so he pricked and prodded and goaded and waited, oh how he waited.

The old woman Margaret was so good at the task she had been given by the previous servant, that he knew, and so all would be well when the time came to take the seven, and that was why he allowed himself this pleasure. It was a risk that the man could somehow warn the boy, but it was a very small risk as he himself was able to manipulate any perception that the boy may experience in such a way that all he would hear would be 'The First Tongue' (the language from the beginning of time). He would never understand it, how could he, he was barely a spec, a being of no worth or significance other than a means to sustain him through the next cycle along with six others from his party. Nothing could prevent what was to be. 'No earthly mortal soul is a match for me,' he thought. After all, it has ever been this way since 'the separation.' This was all part of the balance of things, good needs evil to be good, it's all a counterbalance. His part in the universe was essential, his fee was such a small price to be paid for the status quo. That was how he thought of it.

The Great Being however had thoughts that were entirely different.

Chapter 10

The boy heard the slam of the door downstairs, and the usual fumbling's in the kitchen. If he was lucky, then it would all soon be quiet, and he could sleep. Sleep was what he needed most of the time,. but at night, in bed he was either wide awake and listening like a deer in the forest for the snap of a twig, or the rustle of a leaf. Or he was brutally awakened. He knew the signs, if it went quiet he could sleep fairly secure in the fact that he would be unharmed, but if he heard the crashing of things and cussing, then the outcome was usually very different.

Sleep was never 'rest' for him, it was just some form of closure to one day before the start of the next. There was no joy in it, no relaxation, no peace. These were things that had been lost to him for quite a long time now, and it was a burden that he had learned to bear in his own way. It was not what many would call a good way, but it was his way, and it worked for him. It stopped him going crazy, but it was also very difficult. Nobody knew about the troubles that he had to endure, only his tormentor and himself. He realised very early on that involving others would only make life more intolerable, and so stoically, he suffered in silence, and listened and hoped for small mercies.

On this particular occasion he heard a chair, or maybe it was a table being kicked accompanied by a raised voice. His skin went all cold, and his hair stood on end, was it coming again?

He tensed up expecting for the usual stomp up the stairs. He was waiting for his bedroom door to be flung open. He held his breath, listening intently, there was a scraping sound as if the table or a chair was being dragged across the floor, then it went very quiet.

He listened on, but there was no further sound and then he heard a thump, thump. What was that? What was going on?

To his relief he realised it was merely the sound of boots being dropped on the wooden floor. He heard a click, and then saw the flickering light around his bedroom door frame and realised as he finally exhaled that the tv had been turned on, and so he assumed that the danger was now passed.

He turned over, pulled the sheets up around his ears and closed his eyes. After what felt like hours, but was actually about twenty minutes, he fell into another fitful sleep.

Chapter 11

Colin was awake early that Friday morning. He had experienced a particularly vivid dream about his dad again that night. It was infuriating, a bit like experiencing a small step forward one night, where he awoke the next day with a renewed feeling of positivity only for that to be dashed the very next night when the idea that he woke with the previous day had been dashed overnight.

All he knew so far for certain was that his dad was trying to tell him 'something'. He no longer thought it was about his dad at all. He just wanted to tell Colin something, that was clear now, but what something was it? Sometimes he thought he was trying to warn him, other times just to tell him what to do when he was gone. How to look after his mum, and all that sort of thing. That troubled him greatly of course because there was no way he could listen to that and accept it.

His dad had been in hospital for quite a long time now without much change on the outside, but Colin never got the impression from the doctors and nurses' demeanour or actions that it was anything other than, he will wake up when he is good and ready.

Colin felt that too, it was awkward trying to converse with someone in that state and doubly so when either your mum, or a nurse, was in earshot, and so he said little when others were around, and waited for those moments when they were alone to chat and to ask him what the dreams were, and what was he trying to say. His dad's eyes would flicker and start darting around under their lids as he spoke, and that thoroughly convinced Colin that he understood what was being said to him, and that he desperately wanted to reply, which meant that his brain was OK. So, he was going to come back to them sooner or later. For some reason he couldn't put his finger on it, but Colin really wanted his dad to wake up and talk to him now, specifically before the school trip to Bavaria in a week's time.

His mum was sensing a rising urgency in Colin during their visits to hospital, she could see that, but being a clever boy, he hid it well. She knew nothing of the dreams, and his concerns because when in front of her Colin would pre-empt anything she was about to say with a quick statement.

'Dad looks better today,' or 'I told Dad while you got us a drink about the school trip, and his eyes moved Mum, that's a good sign right?'

He always said just enough at the right time to put her off the train of thought she had, or to forget what she was about to say. This was something he needed to keep to just him and his dad, and try and figure this out alone. 'After all he is just talking to me about this and not mum, so it's a man thing,' Colin thought.

'Eat your breakfast dear,' Mrs Hart said one morning, bringing Colin out of his daydream with a start.

'Sorry Mum, just thinking about school stuff, we get our results today. We find out what school we are all going to.'

'Yes, I'm sure you'll love grammar school,' she said. 'Mrs Cropper tells me it was the making of her boy going there. He's a manager at the big supermarket in town now. I thought when he grew up that the only time he would ever go in there would be to pinch things,' she said. 'He was a proper tearaway at your age Colin. Colin?'

'Er, yeah thanks Mum,' he said not really knowing what she had said at all.

When he got to school there was a sense of apprehension and excitement in the playground.

'Well today's the day,' said Rich. 'I am hoping that I did OK, I wouldn't want you two brain boxes going all boring on me, quoting Shakespeare and stuff,' he said to Colin and Baz.

'I'd explain it all to you mate,' said Baz 'I'd even teach you how to spell his name.'

'Yes very funny...not,' said Rich as he playfully punched him in the arm.

'What about you Col, any thoughts mate?' said Rich.

'Well, I'm sure we will all end up where we should,' he said. 'I just hope that we all end up there together.'

'Well said!' said Steph as she approached with the other girls.

'You lot, will all be going to the girl's grammar anyway,' said Rich 'Especially Briony, or as I like to call her, swot number one.' He said this looking at BB.

She rolled her eyes and said 'I am not a swot!'

'Do you know any Shakespeare?' said Rich

'A little, why?' said BB

'Just curious, we will have to learn that stuff according to Baz if we get to grammar school that is,' said Rich 'So tell us some.'

'Recite,' said Steph looking irritated.

'OK recite us some then,' said Rich

'From what play?' said BB

'The Merchant Of Venice!' said Baz chiming in.

'OK,' said BB who paused and then said

'The quality of mercy is not strained.

It droppeth as the gentle rain from Heaven.

Upon the place beneath.

It is twice blessed,.

It blesseth him that gives, and him that takes.

Portia, Act 4 Scene 1,' she said.

All six of them looked at her agog.

'What?' said BB after a moment.

'That was amazing,' said Rich, 'Seriously BB.'

She blushed and looked away as the school bell rang.

Colin looked across at Steph who was fuming, and he smiled as they went in through the door.

'Settle down you lot,' said Mr Ford 'I have a headache.'

'Too many in The Rising Sun last night Sir?' said a voice from the back quietly.

'Henderson!' screeched Mr Ford.

'It wasn't me Sir, I think it was him,' said Henderson pointing at the full-sized skeleton at the back of the class that was used in biology.

A few giggles erupted.

'Alright, that's enough, register call and then be on your way,' he said.

Chapter 12

At lunch time Mr Ford went to the staff room for a strong coffee and a break from the hubbub that he had endured all morning. His headache hadn't improved much, and so he was intending to have a couple of tablets and just relax for 45 minutes or so.

He opened the door, walked in and the only other person that was in there was the only other teacher in the whole crummy school that he had any personal feeling for. It was Deirdre (Miss Rhymer), they had dated covertly a couple of times as Deirdre did not want to appear 'unprofessional' in front of the other teachers and of also course the Headmaster, Mr Moore.

He didn't really agree with her view, there was nothing in the rules about staff relationships one way or the other, but at first he had gone along with her wishes, and then one night after a couple of pints down the local pub he had been foolish enough to mention it to another male teacher that he and Deirdre were now 'an item.'

'You crafty old dog, well played Derek!' the other teacher had said.

It made him feel good, but then he realised what he had done.

'You can't tell anyone Clive!' said Derek 'Deirdre doesn't want to make it public knowledge just yet, you know how she is.'

'Won't tell a soul old man,' said Clive, and they carried on drinking and talking about other matters.

Well, as everyone knows walls have ears and word travels fast in a place where teacher small talk and gossip are all little nuggets of excitement in a world of rules and regulations, and extra-curricular activities were especially so. It should therefore have been no surprise that two days later 'the cat was out of the bag'. Deirdre, who was a quiet unassuming character, became a whirling dervish as she verbally lambasted poor Derek about his stupidity and lack of respect for her. How foolish he had made her feel, etc. the list went on. All he could do was say 'I'm sorry' to the back of her head as she stormed off.

They had not spoken since and that was over a week ago.

Derek walked into the room, coughed and said, 'Hello Deirdre.'

She ignored him.

After a moment or two he said, 'I apologised, I can't say more than that can I? It just slipped out; we were down the pub and..'

'Men and pubs, and you and your big mouth, I feel such a fool, I can't even look Mrs Hedges in the eye now, and I'm sure some of the kids know. The girls anyway, it is all so embarrassing.' said Deirdre.

'Look I'm really sorry Deirdre, I really am but, they would have all found out eventually so better to be out in the open right at the beginning eh?' he said.

'The point is Derek!' she spat out his name. 'You didn't <u>tell me</u> that you had said anything to anybody, and so when I was confronted with personal questions about you and me, I was totally unprepared, I hummed and hawed and looked like a complete dimwit!' she said.

After a pause Derek said, 'I know I'm an oaf, but we are taking the kids on the school trip together next week, so we have to be able to at least talk to each other.'

'I am talking to you,' said Deirdre who then turned away and started reading a magazine on the table.

'I need a drink, of er coffee that is,' said Derek. He pushed the button on the machine and a paper cup dropped down and started to fill.

'Can we talk Deirdre..please? I am trying here.'

Deirdre got up and walked to the door, stopped and half turned.

'Come round to my flat about 7pm tonight. We can talk then,' and with that she opened the door quickly and whisked away without waiting for a reply.

Derek finished his coffee and went to the form room. It was customary to complete an afternoon register call as well as first thing in the morning and so he opened the door expecting to see all of Form 4C sat at their desks waiting.

They were all there as usual, and also there, was the headmaster with a handful of brown envelopes, which Derek quickly recalled what he had forgotten to mention first thing, and that was that the headmaster would be at afternoon register call to hand out the letters. The letters that would tell the children which schools they would be attending next year. He cursed inwardly then smiled at the headmaster.

'Good afternoon Sir,' he said

'Is it Mr Ford? The pupils look a little surprised to see me almost like they hadn't been told I was coming,' he said keeping a straight face.

'Ah, well you see Sir,' began Derek who was then spoken over.

'No matter,' he said. 'Well children, today is a big day for you all. These letters in my hand hold your future paths. I wish you well and say study hard, listen well and learn. That Is the key to success.'

The headteacher then proceeded to go through the class role call alphabetically by surname and telling them which school they were going to be attending. Even though the letters were sealed, and even though they were supposed to be opened by the parents at home, he had decided to 'inform' them individually in front of all their classmates whether they had passed or failed.

Derek thought this was a rather cheap and poor thing to do, embarrassing the kids in front of each other in this way, but said nothing even though he whispered a name under his breath.

'Brown, girl's grammar. Top marks well done young lady,' he said as he passed Briony her envelope.

'Thank you Sir,' she said.

'Duke B, Duke P' he said to the Duke twins 'Secondary modern both of you.' He practically threw the envelopes at them like they were hot potatoes and moved on.

They did not reply but looked at each other, and also at Keith Henderson and smiled.

'Gold, boy's grammar. Well done lad,' said the Headmaster.

'Thank you Sir,' said Barry as he clutched his envelope proudly.

'Harmon,' he looked at Veronica, 'Secondary modern,' he said.

She took the envelope and looked like she was about to burst into tears. 'Your mark was right on the line Veronica,' he said. 'And so, I have had a word with the Governors at the girl's grammar school, and recommended that they reserve a place there for you if they can. You will find out before the last day of term,' he added.

'Thank you Sir,' she said, as her eyes misted over. All the girls wanted to give her a hug right there and then, but that would have to wait.

'Hart, boy's grammar. Well done lad, difficult year for you boy, so well done indeed,' said the Headmaster.

The gang looked a little puzzled apart from Steph and Rich who knew how things had been of late for Colin and his mum. They both smiled at him.

'Thank you Sir,' said Colin, who felt happy and sad all in one moment. He knew both his parents would be pleased and that feeling overrode the negatives he felt about going to a school in the next town.

'Henderson,' said the Head and paused 'Boy's grammar. Well, I must admit I don't surprise easily, but this is a surprise boy,' he said as he handed Keith Henderson his letter.

All the gang looked at him in amazement. That was not supposed to happen they all thought in unison.

Henderson took his letter, stuffed it under his jumper and mumbled 'Thanks.'

The Dukes looked like they had lost a diamond and found a lump of coal.

'Secret swot!' one Duke said to the other then they looked away in a sulk.

Jenkins, grammar school. Skin of your teeth boy, skin of your teeth. You need to work hard to succeed there, no joking around anymore,' said the Headmaster.

'Thank you Sir,' said Richard as he smiled at Colin and Barry.

'Pritchard, girl's grammar. Well done young lady,' said the Headmaster.

'Thank you Sir,' Steph said as she blushed.

The last member of the gang, Rachel Stiles also got to the girl's grammar. So, they were all in except for 'V', but maybe she will still get a place anyway, they all hoped.

As the girls huddled round V, Baz wanted to go over to her and say something, as he was quite fond of her.

'Leave it to the girls Baz,' said Colin, and so he did, and they all went off to afternoon classes.

Chapter 13

The letter in the envelope meant as much to the boy as anything that he could recall since his mum had died. His dad had coped reasonably well at first, but it hadn't been too long before he had turned to drink as a comfort. He drank more and more, and slowly he became a different person. He had never been a particularly attentive father, but the loss of his wife had sent him down a rabbit hole that he was never going to emerge from, and so he gave up. He gave up on himself, but more importantly, he gave up on his own son. His only son.

At first he was just short with the boy, but one day when he had dared to answer back, the father had cuffed him hard around the ear. It was a shock to both of them. He apologised to the boy at the time, but a few days later, and after a few drinks, he clipped him again, and this time the boy hadn't said a thing he had just dropped something, and that had been enough. It didn't even break it, no damage was done to the object, only to the boy.

It just got worse from there.

When he got home that day, he didn't think that he would say anything or give his father the envelope. He doubted that he even cared, or knew anything about the boy's life anymore. At first the indifference hurt him more than the physical, but now all he cared about was trying to avoid the beatings, get to a good school, obtain a good education there, and then leave. Leave this town, his father, the other kids. Leave them all far behind, and start completely new somewhere else. That thought that goal, sustained him now. Sure, he hadn't made the best of the school he was in, but friends were a luxury he couldn't afford. He didn't want anyone to know what humiliations he had to endure, and so he did his best to push everyone away, it was better that way.

Chapter 14

Derek rang the doorbell and waited. What seemed about five minutes later but was probably only fifty or sixty seconds the door opened, and Deirdre ushered him in with a wave of her hand. He shuffled in a little awkwardly behind her a like a naughty child waiting for, and expecting, another telling off. He had a bottle of red in his hand.

'You know where the corkscrew and the wine glasses are,' said Deirdre as she sat on the sofa.

Her flat had a very open layout, kitchen, living and dining area all in one room. A short corridor at the far end from the front door led to the bathroom and bedroom. The décor was safe, muted colours, apart from a large painting that was a vivid butterfly, all colours of the rainbow and Derek thought it was crudely done and a little out of place. When he first saw it he was just about to say something that he would definitely have regretted later on, but fortune was on his side as he spotted that it had been signed by Deirdre's sister, who had died a few years before in a riding accident, and so he did not comment and forever after always tried not to look at it at all in case Deirdre asked him what he thought of it. He knew that he was not the world's best liar, and so he ignored it. Well ignored it as much as you could do to anything so garish and out of place that is.

With two glasses of wine in hand he went over to the living area and placed them on the two coasters that had appeared upon the coffee table. He sat down.

'I'm sorry that I am an idiot, I know I've already apologised Deirdre, but I really didn't think before I spoke when I told Clive,' he half lied.

'I don't like to be caught off guard or made to look stupid Derek, and you managed to achieve both with your clumsiness,' said Deirdre in a weary resigned sort of way. 'If you had just told me straight away, I would have been prepared.'

This was the real reason she was angry; it wasn't that people knew now; it was that she hadn't been in control of telling them herself.

'I have serious misgivings about coming on the trip with you after this. I was considering asking the Headmaster if Mrs Hobbs could take my place. She speaks German and would be prepared to go I'm sure,' said Deirdre.

'Mrs Hobbs!' he squawked. 'She's an absolute dragon, you can't do this to me Deirdre, it will be a nightmare, she is past retirement age already, and the girls barely know her, and I, well I couldn't bear it, I wouldn't know what to say. She would be telling me off every five minutes in front of the whole lot of them, and I wouldn't be able to say anything would I, I mean she's..old.' He blurted all this out like a machine gun, flailing his arms and then standing up.

He looked at Deirdre who was calmly drinking her wine with a look on her face that he couldn't read.

'Deirdre?' he implored like a small child, 'Please.'

'I said I was considering it, and I have thought it through.' She left it hanging there.

'And what decision have you come to?' Derek gulped.

'I've decided to go. Not for your sake mind. It will be the last time I see the girls, as they will all go off to grammar school next year,' said Deirdre. 'Now sit down and drink you wine.'

And that was where the hostilities ended. Their relationship was not discussed further that evening. They mentioned Veronica though, they both thought she thoroughly deserved a place at the girl's grammar school.

'Even though he's a windbag, I do believe that the Headmaster can swing it, so she gets in,' said Derek.

'I hope so,' said Deirdre. 'I hope so.'

Far away Margaret sensed that the last small hurdle had been overcome and she felt the tension ease in her bony shoulders, she knew that the beast was in control and that the time was very close now. She afforded herself a small glass of wine as she sat there growing older by the second but soon, very soon she would be young once more.

Chapter 15

It was the last Thursday before the end of term in fact the end of the school year. An eventful year for the children in Form 4C, and now they were all going to go their separate ways. Of course, they still had the school trip to Bavaria to look forward to, but after that, it would be different schools, different journeys.

The gang were resigned to the fact of separation. they had discussed it many times now, and they were of one accord when it came to staying in touch. They would see each other evenings and weekends, they would set up a WhatsApp chat group and share things, pictures on Instagram etc. too. These things would all help soften the blow of course, but that shared experience of being 'always together' would be lost somehow, and they all knew it. V was more acutely aware of this, as she was the only one of them who had been given the news in front of the whole class that she had failed, and that hurt, it hurt a lot.

The rest of the gang were of course supportive, trying to put a positive spin on things.

'You'll be top of the class, which would be great wouldn't it?' said Baz

She looked at him and said nothing, her eyes fell, and her bottom lip quivered. He had an overwhelming feeling right then and there to grab her up in his arms, squeeze her tight and tell her everything was going to work out fine.

He didn't do that of course because he was only twelve and that sort of holds you back from throwing yourself into things like that.

'I will do my best to make things right for you,' he thought. 'I really will,' but he didn't say it.

What he said was 'The Headmaster thinks that you will get a place, he said so. I think he is doing all he can, and well I think he'll come through, so don't worry. I know he's a bit well 'headmaster-ish' but I really think he's going to do it.'

V looked at Baz, straight in the eyes and held his gaze, it made his tummy flip a little and his legs felt a little weak.

'Thanks Baz,' she said.

Barry was taken aback because she had never called him Baz before, it was always Barry. He liked it and he smiled at her, and she reciprocated the smile, albeit with tears in her eyes.

The last few days of term were about getting ready for the trip for those that were going from Form 4C, other classes were going to different places but for Form 4C it was Bavaria. The school had never organised a trip there before. In fact, they were fully intending to send Form 4C to the Isle of Wight, but a bunch of paraphernalia had mysteriously arrived a few months previously in several buff envelopes with spiderish writing on them and postmarked from Germany. One was sent to Mr Ford, one to Miss Rhymer and the other to the Headmaster.

Of course, they thought it a little odd that there was no forwarding information, so they had absolutely no idea who had sent it to them.

After a little research (mostly by Deirdre), it was decided that Form 4C would indeed go there for their summer trip. And so it was that the wheels and cogs started to turn that day, and the fate of all the characters that would be involved in the age-old dance were now starting to be inextricably aligned.

That Thursday evening after V got home from school, she found herself thinking about Barry. He had been so kind and thoughtful to her. It wasn't a surprise exactly as he was always nice, but when it was singled out specifically towards her she wasn't sure how she felt about that. She had been thinking about it all day. He had made her feel 'better' which was a minor miracle because it didn't matter what Steph or BB, or even Rach her best friend had said to her, or done for her. Up to that point, she just felt like the world was ending, and what was worse was that she was so annoyed with herself.

She remembered that while she was doing the 12+ exam, there were several multi choice questions and she had a feeling that she had made silly mistakes there. She had whizzed over the questions as they were at the very end of the test, and she hadn't paid them enough attention as she felt that she'd already got it in the bag by that point, but boy had she been wrong! That gnawed away at her, it was very hard to take, or accept. Baz had taken her out of that cycle of malaise that she was in. She had started to think positively again, and she would always be grateful to him for that.

'I am going to do so well there that they will have to let me go to grammar at the end of the first term,' she had thought, (she knew this had been achieved once or twice in the past), but it was a very rare thing indeed.

V's daydream was interrupted by a loud knock at the front door. She heard her mum answer it, and have a conversation with whoever was standing there. She was in her bedroom, so the voices were muted, but it was definitely a man, and the voice was familiar too, but she couldn't quite place it as it was too muffled.

'Veronica!' shouted her mother from the foot of the stairs. 'Letter for you!'

A letter for me she thought, how odd as she opened her door and went downstairs.

Her mother was standing there, the front door was shut, and the visitor had clearly left.

'Who was that Mum?' she said.

'The postman dear. He said that he was on his way back to the depot after his round and he noticed this letter on the floor of his van. It has your name on it but no address, but he knows us anyway of course.'

She handed the envelope to V. It was a buff colour, and her name was written in a spiderish hand on the front. She opened it and read the page that was within.

> **Your place assured**
> **The decision made**
> **It's time to end**
> **This sad charade**
> **Tomorrow morn**
> **You will be told**
> **A place at grammar school**
> **You'll hold.**

V read it aloud to her mum, who then took it to read for herself.

'This is not an official letter, it's a prank. That's really mean, don't get upset Veronica, it's probably that Henderson boy,' she said.

'No, it's OK Mum, really.'

V wasn't sure why she said it was OK, but one thing was certain, no twelve-year-old boy was behind this. She felt calm the rest of the evening and slept well for the first time in days.

Next morning as she entered the school gates there was a lady standing there asking all the girls as they walked in. 'Are you Veronicas Harmon?'

She approached V and asked the same question of her.

'Yes Miss,' she said.

'Then this is for you dear,' the lady said and without waiting for a reply she walked out of the gates got into a large car and drove off.

BB came up to her.

'Do you know who that was?' she said as the rest of the gang huddled round.

'No.' said V.

'Headmistress of the girl's grammar, that's who, I recognized her from the picture in the paper when they were given an award for top girls school in England,' she said.

'What did she give you?' said Steph.

'This letter,' V replied.

'Open it, open it!' said Rach 'Come on, open it.'

She scanned the eager faces and held out the letter to Baz.

'Read it to me please,' she said.

Somewhat surprised he took the envelope from her, and took out the letter. It looked official as it was on letterheaded thick paper. He scanned the wording without a sound.

'Read it aloud, you lemon!' said Rich.

'What is in it? What does it say?' said Colin

'What does it say!' said Baz 'It says everything!' he turned to V with a beam on his face and said 'It's a golden ticket V, you're in, you're going to the girl's grammar school. Apparently they got your mark wrong, you're not in because anyone asked, you are in because you passed!'

He held the letter out and V swiped it up, threw her arms around his neck and gave him the biggest kiss on the lips he had ever had in his life.

The rest of the gang seemed stunned for a second then as one, they linked arms and shouted 'Hooray!' so loudly that all the crows that were sat on the fences nearby took to flight.

As she drove home the headmistress felt like a weight had been lifted off her shoulders. Such dreams she had had these last few days, so vivid, so specific. A force so strong that she could not rest. A feeling of urgency had grown within her, and she finally submitted to what she had been told to do. She had called the school, received the exam test paper of this Veronica Harmon (a girl she did not know) and she remarked her test paper. Several of the questions had been marked 'wrong' incorrectly, she did not know how this could happen, but it had. The girl now had the sufficient grade for a place at her school and so she had made arrangements. She had done as she had been bidden in her dream, and visited the girl personally to give her the letter.

The Hutenghast felt weaker, it had taken much of his remaining strength but all seven had to be there for 'The Refreshing,' and he knew that failure to act now could result in this girl not being at the summoned place at the appointed time.

What the beast did not know however was that this intervention had made no difference. Veronica Harmon, who he was certain was not going to come, because it was one thing too much to bear, was now going to come anyway. The intervention of a boy had changed her thinking. She would have gone now no matter what school she was going to; friends mean everything. A thought that was foreign to the mind of a beast like he, who has no good left within him. So it was that he was now weaker, much weaker than he should have allowed himself to become, for no good reason, but he was also arrogant and confident. All would be well, he knew that, or did he? Maybe it was more hope now than certainty, and that troubled him.

Far away and high above The Great Being saw all things and he was content.

Chapter 16

Colin was pleased for V of course he was. The joy on her face and all his friend's faces too was a real picture. It made him feel good, but he was also very troubled by his dreams about his dad, in fact everything about his dad in general really, but he hid it well as he danced and pranced around with the others.

He was still getting the feeling that his dad was desperate to tell him something important, desperate to wake up. Colin felt the urgency grow as the days passed, like it was heading towards a crescendo of some kind. As the intensity grew he began to think that it was all to do with one of two things. It was either something to do with going to a new school or it was about the trip to Bavaria. The unease of it made him feel like he should change school, or cancel going on the trip. As he mulled it all over, he realised that it could not possibly be about the new school. His mum and dad desperately wanted him to get to grammar school, and so if he ditched that, it would be crazy. It didn't make any sense, and besides his mum would never allow it, and his dad would kill him when he woke up!

'No,' he thought. 'This is about the trip; it's got to be. But why? It was just a school trip. They weren't even flying there, it was on a coach, so no real danger of a crash. Maybe someone was going to have an accident there, a fall or something, or there was going to be an avalanche.' Then he remembered that avalanches don't happen in the summertime.

And so, he decided that whatever it was, he would keep an eye out for his friends, not let anyone do anything too risky, and then everything would be OK.

He wished his dad could wake up now, before they went, and tell him what troubled him so much. But you can't always have what you want when you want it. One miracle today was good enough, and today's miracle was 'V's and he was pleased, so pleased. Whatever lay ahead, trips, new schools, growing up. Growing apart was not an option. This was going to be his purpose.

He had seen from his mum and dad that staying in touch with old friends, school mates, holiday acquaintances, previous work colleagues etc. always seem to revolve around just one person. One person who made the effort, who emailed everyone, who arranged get togethers or short breaks away. All that sort of thing.

On his mum's side, she was the one that appeared to do all that arranging and keeping in touch stuff. She still saw a handful of her school friends regularly, and she had morphed some ex-work colleagues in with them along the way too. She was good at that, keeping it all going.

His dad was different, his mate from school Pete, he was the 'doer' in his dad's life outside of couples that is, as his mum kept in contact with them. There were three of them in his dad's gang (the third guy was called Nick who always referred to them as the Three Amigos), they met up two or three times a year, so it wasn't as intense or hands on as mum's friendships, but it worked for them. They saw each other, and it was unwritten but known that they were always there for each other if push came to shove (Pete and Nick had been to see his dad every week since he had been in a coma, laughing and joking in the room and telling him he owed them a crate full of beer etc.).

Proper mates thought Colin. Me and Rich and Baz are going to be like that. He fully expected BB to manage the girl's side, she was the dynamo there and Steph would make sure they all meet up from time to time (the thought never entered Colin's head that he and Steph would ever lose contact). He wasn't going to let that happen.

So, in the future he was going to be more like his mum than his dad in that way. 'Friends are everything,' he thought on that balmy Friday, the last day of school. The trip was only a few days off now and he'd be ready. He wouldn't let his dad down, or his mates, even though he had no clue what was ahead.

Part II

Chapter 17

Every boy and girl from Form 4C were up bright and early on the day of the trip to Bavaria.

V had been like a live wire ever since she had received the news about grammar school. The trip for her only a few days previously had held little appeal as she knew that it would be hard to take, she would be seeing all the gang enjoying themselves, so excited about the trip and their new schools with her being the proverbial odd one out. 'Nightmare!' she had thought. Not now though, she couldn't wait.

Rach had been almost as upset as she had been, and although that was great, it had also made her so much more emotional about the whole thing.

'Thank goodness that is now ancient history,' she thought. 'This trip is going to be the best.'

Rach was up earlier than everybody else. Her little life revolved around the friendship with the gang and most of all with V and what had seemed an utter disaster a few days ago now seemed like a perfect dream ending. She had thought it was quite weird, the whole thing about the headmistress rechecking V's marks and all that, but her natural curiosity had quickly fallen away when she realised that V was actually coming with her to girl's grammar (or GG as they now called it). This was such fantastic news and she had been just as thrilled as V to hear it.

Steph was packed and ready to go two days before as was her way.

There was preparation, and then there was 'Steph Prep' as the gang had nicknamed it. Her uncanny ability to think of every conceivable eventuality, and prepare for it like she was some astronaut about to go into space. She planned for everything that she did at 'Olympic level,' that was how Rich had said it to her one time when they were all going on a school visit to the local cinema to see a film about a boy and his kestrel.

She had drinks, food, sweets, a torch, spare battery, tissues etc. the list went on. 'Blimey,' Colin had said to her. 'If you've got a tent in your backpack and it rains in the cinema is it big enough for seven?' She smiled as she thought of it over her breakfast.

Colin himself was conflicted as was increasingly the way in recent months. He wanted to enjoy the trip and be with his friends too, he was looking forward to the new school of course as they all were, but he also worried about his mum being on her own. He worried about his dad and the dreams constantly too. He had really wanted him to wake up before the trip, but that hadn't happened and so he was already mentally preparing himself for whatever was going to 'go wrong' on this trip.

'Don't worry Dad,' he thought to himself as he ate his cooked breakfast. 'I've got this.'

As for the rest of the gang, Rich just wanted to have a laugh with Colin and Baz mostly but also he wanted to spend time talking to BB.

Briony herself wanted to drink in all the culture, she knew the names of every place they were going to, what the scenery was like, what to see, she had done her research thoroughly.

Baz was just content to be with his mates. He was uncomplicated in that way, happy in his world, but this trip was a little different to the norm as he also wanted to spend more time with V.

Everyone arrived at the school in dribs and drabs. The weather was fine, and they milled around in the playground waiting for the coach which was supposed to leave at 8am. It was 7:45am and no coach was to be seen.

BB looked across at Mr Ford and Miss Rhymer. They looked a little on edge and she presumed it was because of the coach, or rather the lack of a coach.

'I reckon that they've had a tiff,' a voice said, and BB turned around to see Steph coming over to her.

'Do you really think they are an item?' she said.

'Yes, on and off,' said Steph with a grin, and they both laughed.

'Did you check with the travel firm yesterday about the coach arriving at 7:30am like I asked you to?' Deirdre said to Derek.

'Yes of course,' he lied. 'It's probably just caught in traffic,' he gulped.

'There would not be any traffic at this time of the day,' she said, 'Something must be wrong.'

'No, it's all fine Miss,' said Barry who had been ear wigging on their conversation. 'There it is, look!' He pointed to the coach as it rounded the corner.

'There, see!' said Derek trying to hide the squeak in his voice as he spoke.

He cleared his throat. 'OK children, get your things and line up. Boys behind me, girls behind Miss Rhymer,' he said.

There was a scuffling of feet and dragging of bags as they all did what they were told.

Keith Henderson and the Duke twins had been waiting for this command and were front of the queue. 'Back seat,' Henderson said to the twins (boys always want to sit on the back seat so they can pull faces at the traffic behind them).

'I say we sit as near to the driver as we can,' BB said to the gang. 'That way we can keep an eye on things.'

'So, it's got nothing to do with being as far away as possible from the Back Seat Boys then,' said Rich as he jerked his thumb in their direction.

Everybody except Henderson and the Dukes laughed at that, even the teachers (with their hands over their mouths). Henderson's face flushed and the twins looked annoyed, but they said nothing, they just looked ominous.

Colin eyed Rich who was completely oblivious to their rage. He was so cool about that sort of thing. 'I doubt whatever is going to happen on this trip will happen to Rich,' thought Colin but all the same he would remain vigilant.

The coach was white with a yellow stripe down the side and bore the emblem Watts Coaches (We'll get you there). I hope it does thought Deirdre as she read it. She always worried about things going wrong.

The air brakes hissed as the coach came to a stop and the driver opened the door with a switch in the cab and hopped out.

'You're late!' said Deirdre.

'Am I?' he said smoothing his moustache with his hand.

He was a short stocky man of about forty with dark brown/black hair and a Mediterranean complexion. He looks like the Super Mario guy thought Derek and the large moustache only added to that look. A couple of the boys mumbled something to each other and sniggered. Derek said nothing as he realised that about half of all the boys thought the exact same thing as him and the sniggering pair did, and that thought lightened his mood a little. Last night's tension with Deirdre was all but forgotten in that moment. She still hadn't completely forgiven him for blabbing, and he had recently been getting a little tired of walking on eggshells all the time, and so when he finally told Deirdre to 'Brighten up and stop looking so miserable,' earlier on, it hadn't gone down very well.

The driver proceeded to grab all the children's bags and stow them away as they all got on board. Henderson and the twins raced to the back seat as the other children took the nearest available seats to the front. The coach was not full and so the four rows directly in front of the back seat were all empty.

'Lonely back there?' said Rach, who was secretly quite fond of Keith Henderson, although she wasn't sure why, and she had never told a soul about it, even V didn't know. She thought he liked her too, but she was never quite certain, as he was so horrible most of the time. Something told her that it was just an act. She didn't know why he behaved as he did, but she somehow thought he was OK underneath all the prickly exterior.

Keith Henderson said nothing in reply but one of the twins said, 'Shut it Nobby.'

'Leave it,' hissed Keith under his breath.

Shortly afterwards, the coach was ready to go. The driver had shut the lower doors with a loud clunk to secure the stowage, and the crows had once again taken flight at the sound of it.

He boarded the coach at 8:25am and got in the cab. 'Hoff we go,' he said, (even Deirdre smiled at that).

'Super Mario,' thought Derek as he settled back into his seat.

The engine rumbled into life and the coach moved off. All the children automatically looked out of the window at the school as they left.

'You know what?' said Baz after a few moments. 'That's the last time we will ever be all together here at this school, in that playground.'

Nobody said a word, not even the twins. This trip was the final chapter of their old lives, the new was just around the corner and for just a fleeting moment they were all as one.

Chapter 18

The coach was comfortable enough although it appeared to be quite old. The seats looked like they had been re-covered recently, and they were adequately spaced too so the children settled down quickly. They started to chat amongst themselves about whatever was on their minds at the time. Everyone was still quite buzzed with excitement, and so the noise levels were relatively high, with sporadic laughs and screeches plus the odd shout. This would probably have commanded a response from the teachers under normal situations but the vibrations and noise levels of the old coach itself with its whining gearbox and back axle along with the large thumping diesel motor mostly cancelled these noises out, and so they sped along at about 50mph without too much fuss.

'I am a bit worried that this coach may break down in the Alps or something,' Deirdre said to Derek quietly enough for the children behind them not to overhear. 'I would have thought that a newer coach would be supplied.'

'It's only got to get us to Munich Deirdre, remember? It's all hiking and local buses from there. The coach will leave us in Munich and in 10 days' time we will be picked up from there again at the coach station. We will probably be in a different coach entirely on the way back,' Derek informed her. 'Had you forgotten?'

'No, but the local transport may be older, worse even,' she moaned.

Derek was about to reply when the driver turned his head and spoke (he had obviously been listening to their entire conversation despite the background noise levels).

'I stay,' he said.

'I beg your pardon?' said Deirdre.

'I stay in Germany, wait for you, then come back to meet you again. I visit my sister; she lives in Stuttgart. I see her last 5 years ago. She's very excited, me too,' he continued.

'I see, very nice,' said Derek and looked away to continue his conversation with Deirdre in an even quieter voice.

'There you see,' Derek said to Deirdre. 'It's all in hand.'
'Hmm!' she said.

Derek took that as a conversation closer, he looked around to make sure all the children were sat down properly and then opened his book to read.

'Who is Gareth Edwards?' said a voice from behind them. Both Deirdre and Derek looked round to see Richard Jenkins looking at them between the two headrests.

'It's rude to read over somebody else's shoulder Richard,' said Deirdre.

'Sorry Miss,' said Rich as he continued to look at Derek.

'He's a, was, a rugby player, for Wales,' Derek said. 'One of the greatest, probably the greatest,' he said.

'What better than Jonah Lomu?' said Rich.

'Well, maybe or maybe not, different eras you see,' said Derek

'So would Lomu have smashed him then?' he continued.

'Err, sit down and mind your manners boy, it's a long trip so I suggest you rest your brain for a while,' said Derek hotly.

Rich slunk away and spoke to Colin who was sat beside him. 'He's easy to wind up,' he said.

Colin was looking out of the window not really listening until he got a nudge in the arm.

'I said, he's easy to wind up old Fordy,' Rich repeated. 'What's wrong with you anyway you've been quiet ever since we left school. Did you want to sit next to Steph or something?' he goaded with a grin.

That got Colin's attention.

'I can't mate she's sitting next to your girlfriend.'

Rich looked around to see Steph and BB deep in conversation. He turned round, sat down and didn't say another word until they were practically on the ferry.

Adjacent to Colin and Rich sat Baz, he was always the third one in their relationship and that was OK with him. He was not a needy boy; he didn't crave attention like Rich did, and so he was quite happy with his little role. Colin had always been the stable one of the three, the one who kept everything in place because under any other circumstance Baz and Rich would probably not be close friends at all, as they were very different.

They both had a bond or affinity with Colin though and over the years at infant school and junior school they had become firm friends also.

Baz was in the seat alone reading a book, but he was also listening in on the conversation between V and Rach who were sat immediately behind him.

'I still find it hard to believe,' V said to Rach.

'Find what hard to believe?' she replied.

'That we are both going to GG next year, I have to admit I was a nightmare at home about it all, so my mum says anyway.'

'You're always a nightmare,' said Rach with a grin.

'No, seriously, this is the best, you, me, BB and Steph all together.'

'I don't want to burst your bubble, but we will probably all be in different forms anyway,' said Rach 'They do that my dad says, so that you integrate with kids from other schools.'

'Well maybe so, but we will be in lots of classes together and stuff, anyway I'm glad that's all,' said V. 'So, what do you reckon about the boys all getting into grammar, good eh? It's a shame Keith Henderson is going to be there too.'

'That's a mean thing to say! He has the right to the best education the same as the rest of us doesn't he? Just because he is not our friend, doesn't mean that he doesn't deserve his place. He passed the exam didn't he?' Rach replied a little too hotly she realised.

'Gosh, OK, whatever,' said V taken aback a little. 'Why are you fighting his corner, is there something you want to get off your chest?' she said with a mischievous look on her face.

'Don't be ridiculous,' Rach replied, 'I just think if you pass an exam, well you pass an exam that's all,' she said as she looked out of the window to hide her blushing cheeks. 'Kill the subject,' she thought to herself.

'So, what about you know who and that' K.I.S.S,' she mouthed to V.

'It was just the excitement, you know, the spur of the moment,' said V flustered.

'It looked more than that,' said Rach.

'Well, I think you are carrying a little thing for someone at the back of the C.O.A.C.H,' she said as a deflection.

They both looked into each other's eyes for a few seconds to gauge what was really going on in there. They knew each other so well, no secrets. They both realised without words the truth of it, giggled, nodded knowingly at each other, and sat back quietly.

A minute or two later V said, 'You're nuts d'you know that?'

'Takes one to know one,' said Rach.

Baz who had heard nearly everything smiled as he read his book.

Behind Colin and Rich sat Steph and BB. Neither of them were quite as tuned into each other as Rach and V but they were pretty close. Steph hid her feelings for Rich pretty well she thought, and also her irritation at Rich's obvious infatuation with Briony, even though BB herself seemed to be quite oblivious. She did however have a feeling that Colin saw the whole thing, and that was kind of weird, but she didn't mind, she trusted him implicitly and they had known each other like forever.

They didn't speak much on the journey to Dover to catch the ferry. BB had her nose into some travel book about Germany, and Steph ran through everything in her mind. Had she forgotten anything, she did a mental checklist ticking everything off. Finally, she came to the conclusion that she had everything in hand, 'Steph Prep was functioning as it should,' she thought to herself with a smile.

The journey to Dover took a couple of hours.

'I can see the sea!' exclaimed one of the Duke twins as they neared the coast, it was their first visit to the seaside and the excitement got the better of him.

Many of the children laughed and he immediately wanted to hit someone but who? Even though he never appeared to be one of the cleverest of boys, he knew further action, or outburst, would only make him look more stupid, and so he kept his head down. Soon they were at the port entrance.

'We are heres!' exclaimed the driver as if they couldn't see for themselves.

Deirdre stood up and turned around to face the children.

'OK, everyone,' she said. The children mostly carried on with their chattering.

'ATTENTION,' she said.

They all stopped and looked at her (even Derek).

'We are at the port now so be ready to exit the bus if necessary. Hopefully passport control will just look at your passports and do a head count but be prepared please. I have your passports as you know, so no need to leave your seats unless instructed to do so. Clear?'

'Yes Miss,' they all chimed.

The yellow and white coach joined a queue of lorries and other coaches as instructed by a man waving a wand of some sort. The children watched on intently (apart from Steph and a couple of the other children who were seasoned travellers like her). After about 10 minutes a man in a dark blue uniform came to the door of their coach and tapped the glass. As he climbed the steps Deirdre stood up.

'Passports,' he said in a flat tone.

Deirdre handed him the children's' passports and he counted them. He then proceeded to walk slowly down the coach counting all the heads to the left. When he got to the rear of the coach he looked at the three boys on the back seat and winked, then without a word he walked back to the front counting all the heads on the right side of the coach. During this performance none of the children (or teachers) spoke or moved. He had seen this many times before and the little power trip was always a bonus to his day. He then opened each passport and called the name out. As the answer of 'here' came back he checked the passport photo. When he had called all the children's names had been called out he asked Deirdre and Derek to show him their passports also, and they duly obliged. He looked at them and handed Derek his passport and was just about to hand Deirdre hers too when he looked at it again.

'Oh dear,' he said

'What's wrong?' said Deirdre.

'Your passport has expired Miss,' he said.

'What!' she squawked. 'That's not possible, I checked, I'm sure it's got a year left on it.'

'Without even checking it again he said, 'so it has,' with a sly grin. 'My apologies.'

He handed the passport back and said, 'Enjoy your trip.'

Deirdre felt faint and sat down. Then Derek turned to the driver and said, 'Why didn't he check your passport?'

'He did, last week, I cross over many times. This man he always makes the jokes about passport out of date. He is a funny man, no?'

'No, he is definitely not funny!' said Deirdre 'I'm going to report him!'

'Let it go,' said Derek 'He's just a jobs worth.'

During this little conversation between Derek and Deirdre the man from the Port Authority had walked to the next coach that was directly behind them. As he tapped on the window he looked across at Keith Henderson and the Duke twins and winked at them once more. They laughed and Keith said to the twins 'Cool guy that.' They nodded in agreement.

Chapter 19

The week leading up to the school trip had been reasonably quiet. His father had been in a reasonable mood which was always a good thing as that meant that he didn't have to be on edge all the time, like he was ready for anything. He could relax a little for once which was a good feeling, it was a respite in a storm but nevertheless it was welcome. Of course, he had been busy getting all his things organised, he knew that he was very lucky to have a valid passport from the time when he had gone to Spain for a week with his mum and dad, back when he had been nine years old. It was a good thing that it was valid too, as he doubted that his father would have been prepared to organise a new passport for him in time to go on this trip. Spain had been a good holiday, but of course he was completely unaware at the time that his mother was already seriously ill, and that this holiday was to be 'the trip abroad holiday' for them as a family while she was still well enough to travel. It was special because they had never been abroad as a family before, and it had been absolutely perfect in his eyes at the time, his parents seemed happy, they doted on him as he did on them also, but although the Spanish skies were so blue that week, dark clouds were on the horizon for them, the sea change was coming, and nothing would ever be the same again for him or indeed his dad.

For the trip, his dad had given him some spending money, just enough. He said thank you for it, even though he knew that it was a requirement of the trip that the children took a certain amount with them, and so he thought that that was why he had given it to him. It was not out of caring, or love, no it was necessary so that he could be rid of him for 10 days. Well, that is what he thought, but the fact was that his dad was so changeable and difficult to understand that it was impossible to know what was really on his mind at any given time, and long ago he had learned that not asking questions was the best policy.

And so it was that father and son still cohabited in the family home, but communicated very little anymore.

His passport was quite dog-eared considering it had only been used once before. It wasn't because it had been damaged on purpose, or chewed by a dog, no nothing like that. He often held it in his hands as he lay in bed at night thinking of his perfect holiday, his mum, his life as it was. He stared at the boy in the photo, and it was like looking at a stranger. It was him of course, but it wasn't him at the same time. Back then he was happy, popular at school, his world was a good one, but he had morphed into some creature over the months and years. His protective armour was keeping people at a distance, safer that way, he was not prepared to share his misery with any school friends, and so he pushed them all away. When he lay alone at nights with his mind wandering, he felt regrets for the loss of his friends, as well as his mum's departure, but in the cold light of day with the flick of a switch he became a different person, aloof, difficult, hard to understand, just like his dad.

They were very alike, the boy knew that, he also knew that he was making the same mistakes with how he was dealing with this life curve ball, but it seemed the only way for him to survive it until he was old enough to leave home for good and go his own way. Then it would be different, he would be like he was before. At least he hoped he would be like he was before as he lay there clutching his passport night after night with salty tears in his eyes, but when he was awake, at school, living his 'daytime life' as he thought of it, being the way he was now was fun, it felt quite good being mean. He didn't understand how or why he was the way he was, but whatever the reason, he realised that it helped him to cope. It was a mechanism of sorts, but he also he felt a little like that man in an old black and white film that he had watched once where the guy was good during the day and bad at night, he was like him only in reverse. Dr Jekyll during his 'night-time life' Mr Hyde during the day.

The night before the trip his dad had come home late, the boy had made his own dinner that evening which had amounted to little more than cheese on toast and some biscuits. His dad had come home extra late after closing time and the noises that the boy heard downstairs indicated to him that he was not going to have a good night's sleep at all.

He put his passport in with his travelling stuff and lay there waiting. After a few minutes of stomping around downstairs he heard his dad climb the stairs and hover by his door.

'You asleep boy?' he said.

The boy did not reply.

'Well, I'll be asleep when you go in the morning so be quiet, you hear?' he said then walked towards his own bedroom.

As he walked away the boy thought that he heard his father say, 'Have a good trip boy, and keep away from danger,' but he couldn't be sure of it. It certainly didn't sound like something his father would say to him whilst he was under the influence, but stranger things had happened before, and even stranger things were about to happen too.

Chapter 20

The short drive through and onto the ferry bound for Calais was quick and uneventful, apart of course from the entertaining view that the children had of Deirdre slowly coming down from her anger mountain about her passport as Derek pacified her.

'I'd be angry too if a man said anything like that to me,' BB said to Steph. 'It was rude and unnecessary.'

'I thought it was kind of funny,' said Rich poking his head through the headrest behind.

'Your opinion is not relevant,' said Steph, 'You think everything is funny.'

'You're not,' said Rich.

'Not what,' replied Steph.

'Funny, either of you,' he replied, 'I hope you are going to cheer up soon because neither of you have said a word for like an hour, Is there anything wrong?'

'No!' they both chimed together. 'I just thought that man was, was,' stumbled BB.

'Rude and unnecessary?' said Colin appearing around the back of his chair.

'Exactly, thank you Colin, I wouldn't expect him to understand,' BB said looking keenly at Rich who just returned her gaze with a smile until she looked away.

The boys turned back around, and Rich said to Colin, 'We're going to enjoy this trip mate, you wait and see, best ever, guaranteed.'

'I hope so,' said Colin with a faraway look in his eye.

'Don't look so serious Col.' said Rich 'We've got ten days away and then the rest of the summer hols to enjoy before we all go off to a new school together. The girls will cheer up soon enough I'm sure. I think those two have just had a tiff or something, you know what they are like.'

Colin knew the Steph-BB-Rich dynamics here very well, but it had all completely escaped Rich and also BB to a certain extent too. Rich was not exactly Mr Perception, and BB was quite self-absorbed. Steph on the other hand, well time would tell how this all worked out with her, but he had bigger things to concern himself with on this trip. That was something however that he would be keeping to himself until it was all over and done, then maybe he would address things that needed to be addressed before the summer was over.

'Yes, a tiff, I expect so,' he replied as the coach drove up the ramp and into the belly of the ferry.

When all the vehicles were aboard and the large steel doors had been closed Derek looked at the driver inquisitively, and he duly nodded in response.

'OK, boys and girls,' he said. 'Listen up. Please make a note of where we are should you get lost; we are currently in lower deck C1. The coach will be locked up for the duration of the crossing which will take approximately 90 minutes. That gives you all plenty of time to explore, have a drink and a bite to eat in the café. Please do not go anywhere that is marked Staff Only,' he said looking down to the very rear of the coach. 'We will all meet up in the café at 12;45pm, clear?'

'Yes Sir,' they all chimed.

'OK, only take what you need and leave everything else onboard,' he said

Deirdre stood up 'Single file everyone as you go up the stairs to the right,' she said pointing to a door with a sign above it that said Upper Decks. 'Please do not run or rush up the steps, they are steel and could be slippery, we do not want any grazed knees or twisted ankles do we?'

'No Miss,' they said as they all followed Derek off the coach. Deirdre waited until the last child had stepped down into the hold and followed. The final three to exit were of course Keith Henderson and the Duke twins. As he passed her Keith Henderson said, 'Funny man that passport guy eh Miss?' The twins sniggered.

Deirdre looked him dead in the eye and said, 'I am watching you very closely this trip. If there are any problems resulting from your antics I will personally ensure that your parents will be told of it, do I make myself clear Mr Henderson?' she said.

'Yes..Miss,' he replied sheepishly as he got off the coach and she followed behind.

Only the driver was left on board now. 'I like driving the coach, you can keep the teaching,' he said to himself as he rolled a cigarette ready to take up to the upper deck and smoke over an espresso. 'Kids, they are so much trouble,' he said, 'I like it just me and my driving, I don't want twenty children on holidays, no fun, just work!' He smiled as the door closed behind him and he started up the steps along with the others.

Even though it was a nice day, there was quite a breeze blowing up there on the outside decks, and as the children wandered around they huddled together and pulled their collars close to their necks as their hair blew around in the wind and their eyes began to water. They were all genuinely excited now of course, even the back seat boys were, but they hid it well enough.

The gang naturally gravitated towards each other as they always did. All seven stood there looking out across the turgid water towards France, at the other ship and boats, and also at the seagulls and petrels as they wheeled around in the sky.

'Well, here we all are,' said Baz breaking the silence. 'What a year eh.'

'Very eloquent mate,' said Rich.

'Shut up,' said V. 'This is important, here we all are embarking on one last venture together and then we all go our separate ways, right?'

'Not exactly, at least we are all going to be in the same town, at schools right next door to each other now,' Rach replied as she looked across at V.

'Yes absolutely,' said Steph. 'So, let's all just have fun and enjoy this trip together.'

'You're right,' said Colin

'What about?' said BB, 'This being important, or just having fun?'

'Both,' he replied. 'School was the best days of his life my dad said, er says. Cherish them, he always tells me because they go by in a flash.'

The seven looked at each other quietly and then the moment passed.

'It's freezing out here!' said BB 'Let's go inside to the café and have a hot drink and look at the itinerary.'

'Now there's a plan, can't wait,' said Rich.

The girls all groaned and rolled their eyes, and then they all laughed together as they went back through the weather-beaten doors and into the relative warmth of the corridor. They walked off towards the café, which was in the centre of the ferry.

Keith Henderson, who had been loitering near them all this time watched as they went off. Rach shot him a look and half smiled as she turned and walked away with the others. He hesitated a moment and then went over to the Duke twins who were throwing litter into the sea. 'Let's get a drink, I'm bored out here,' he said, and inside they went. Only Derek and Deirdre were left outside now, they were at the stern of the ferry and were sat on a wooden bench.

'I'm glad you came,' Derek said to Deirdre.

'Relieved you mean,' she replied.

'No, it's got nothing to do with Mrs Hobbs,' he said.

'I'm just glad that you are here, we are here, together.'

'Yes well, I need to look after my girls don't I?' she said. 'While they are still my responsibility that is.'

'I suppose so, don't tell anyone this, but basically they are all good kids really,' said Derek.

'Even Keith Henderson?' said Deirdre.

'The boy has problems at home, single parent and all that. His mum died about three years ago so the Headmaster tells me,' said Derek, 'I wouldn't think of him too harshly, but the Duke twins well that's different. If they make it to thirty without going to prison I will be very impressed!' he said.

'You can't say that Derek!' she said whilst also thinking that she had maybe been a little too harsh on Keith Henderson earlier on.

'Sorry, it's already out there,' said Derek with a grin. 'Come on, I'll buy you a coffee, you probably need one.'

'That I do,' she said. They got up and went inside leaving only the birds to brave the wind. They didn't seem to mind.

Margaret could feel movement, the seven were coming, the time was near. She was all prepared, every detail was just as it should be, nothing could go wrong now. The Hutenghast was also aware that the seven were on the water, it pleased him, it took the concern away, Margaret had been a useful tool to him, and she would not fail him, she could not afford to fail him. He laughed but nobody could hear it.

The Great Being saw all these things and he was content.

Chapter 21

The journey across the channel passed without incident and at 12;45pm they all congregated in the café. A quick count of heads confirmed that they had all survived the trip.

'OK, everyone, have we all got everything with us that we brought on board?' said Derek.

'Yes Sir.'

'OK then, back to the coach,' he boomed as he turned around and they all followed him in a line with Deirdre at the rear.

In the corner of the café sat the coach driver. He laughed to himself, shook his head and followed the troupe out and down the stairs back to the coach.

'Strasbourg,' said BB as they all sat down.

'What about Strasbourg?' said Rich.

'That is where we stop for the night tonight. Did you not listen to what I said in the café?' she replied. 'It's on the French German border.'

'Oh yeah, Strasbourg, that's like another four hours on the coach, right?' he said.

'Six hours,' said Colin.

'Blimey who's idea was it to come on this trip anyway,' Rich groaned.

'Well, it's quite a story really,' said BB. 'Apparently, originally we were going to go to the Isle of Wight but then some random brochures came to the school out of the blue, and they were also sent to Miss Rhymer, at home. They were all about Bavaria, where to go, what to do, everything.'

'That's very interesting,' mused Colin.

'Is it?' said Rich.

'Yes,' he replied as he thought about his dad and all the dreams. 'This is weird Dad,' he thought. 'Very weird.'

Everyone was now on the coach and had sat down, another quick head count by Derek confirmed that they were all on board.

'OK, hoff we go,' said Super Mario as he put the coach in gear and followed the stream of vehicles out and into the port of Calais.

'Will we get another passport man?' said V to the teachers.
'No, we are good to go I think,' said Derek looking across at Super Mario for assurance.

He nodded and they drove off, out into the Calais traffic and Southeast towards Strasbourg which was around 500 miles away.

'OK, settle down,' said Deirdre over the noise of the children talking. 'It's a long way to Strasbourg, I have some reading material if anybody wants something to pass the time.' A couple of the girls put their hands up, and one of the boys also.

Soon everyone had settled back into their seats, and the coach was galloping along, munching up the miles on the motorway towards their destination for the night.

Strasbourg was a fine place, very gothic, steeped in history and laying on the banks of The Rhine. This was all lost on the children of course as they were mostly asleep now after a six-hour journey across France.

The coach pulled into the entrance of The Holiday Inn in Strasbourg which was very close to the water. The children had all been advised in the paperwork pack they received from the school that they were to keep in their hand luggage some toiletries and one complete change of clothing. As Steph looked out the window she smiled to herself, her hand luggage had within it enough provision for about three days. Steph Prep was still working perfectly.

'OK children, we are now at the overnight stop,' said Deirdre. 'I will go and book us all in. In the meantime, please gather all your things and I will be back in a couple of minutes or so.' She exited the coach and walked off towards the reception with the relevant paperwork in her hand. Steph and BB watched her as she walked away.

'She's almost as prepped as you are,' BB said to Steph.

'You mean almost as clued up as you are,' Steph retorted.

They both laughed and grabbed their belongings in readiness.

Fifteen minutes or so passed by and eventually Deirdre reappeared and walked back to the coach.

'Alright children gather your belongings and follow me,' she said.

They all did as they were told and followed her across the gravel driveway and into the hotel foyer with Derek following along at the rear. When they were all safely inside Deirdre handed a piece of paper and a bunch of room key cards to Derek. 'Mr Ford has the boys' key cards here and I have the girls' key cards. If you could go with Mr Ford please boys, he will get you organised, and I will take the girls with me. We are on level one girls and the boys on level two.' Off we go,' she said, and they all walked towards the two large lifts that would take them all up to their rooms.

'Left lift girls, right lift boys,' said Derek.

'This is like being in the army,' said Baz, and they all laughed.

'Just keeping it as easy as possible boy,' said Derek. 'The sooner we get your rooms sorted out the quicker we can all go and have dinner,' he said. 'Does that sound like a plan?'

Can't argue with that,' said one of the Duke's, 'I'm starved.'

'Starving,' said Steph. 'I'm starving,' she corrected him.

'I think we all are after that journey, come on lads,' said Colin averting a potential altercation occurring. He could see that Brian Duke was just about to kick off and say something nasty to Steph. 'No drama, no fuss, just keep it together,' he thought. Partly this was because he was just making sure that the trip went well, but mostly he didn't want to see anyone upset Steph deliberately, that was a big no-no in his book. It didn't matter if it was Brian or Peter Duke (who were the biggest boys in the class) or anyone else for that matter. He had Steph's back, always had, always would, end of.

The lifts opened with a ping, and they all piled in, eleven on each side. The doors closed again and up they went.

The coach driver who had been hanging back just looking on and occasionally shaking his head, took his key from the desk clerk on reception and went up the stairs to the third floor, he didn't like lifts. Once inside his room he proceeded to order his meal from room service, and then went out onto the balcony and lit another cigarette and watched the city of Strasbourg in the fading light of evening.

Back in the lift a voice said, 'Level one, doors opening,' and the doors opened. Deirdre stepped out and handed the keys to the girls in turn.

Room 102 was to be Steph and BB's room, Room 104 was for V and Rach, the other six girls were all given their keys in turn then Deirdre showed them all how to open the door correctly.

'OK girls, down to the dining room in ten minutes please, remember to have your key with you before you close the door.'

'Yes, thank you Miss Rhymer,' said BB and the others replied with 'Thank you Miss.'

Deirdre's room was 120 at the far end of the corridor. 'I will check that out later,' she thought as she got back in the lift and went down to the ground floor to find the restaurant.

Derek and the boys were on level two now, all the keys had been handed out. Colin and Baz were sharing, the Duke twins were sharing (obviously), and Rich had been dumped with Keith Henderson. He did not look happy.

'Please Sir,' he said pulling Derek to one side.

'Save it Jenkins, it is one night boy.' He whispered, although it was obvious that Keith Henderson would be able to hear this conversation.

It was embarrassing and uncomfortable even for Rich, who was pretty thick skinned, so he dropped the subject, and they all went to their prospective doors.

'Dinner in the restaurant in ten minutes,' said Derek as he wandered down the corridor to find his own room.

Rich opened the door and walked in. The room was simple but adequate with two single beds, a desk and chair, sideboard with tv above and a small sofa with a coffee table much like you would find in any hotel twin room anywhere.

'Can I take the bed by the window,' said Keith Henderson.

'Sure, whatever,' said Rich as he thumbed through the pamphlet about the hotel, not reading it as such, just using it as a prop, a diversion, a means not to have a conversation.

Keith Henderson sat on the bed and looked out of the window. 'He is always quiet when he doesn't have Tweedle Dum and Tweedle Dee in tow,' Rich thought and that suited him just fine. He didn't want to talk anyway.

The stupid thing was that they used to be quite good friends once, but that changed a few years ago now when Keith became quiet practically overnight, and started avoiding everyone. Then the Duke twins turned up a couple of years ago. Their father was in a prison nearby, and so they had moved close by with their mum, closer to where he was incarcerated that is, to make life easier for them all. Keith and the Dukes had then become a trio, due to their mutual misery, even though it was not spoken of. Rich was also unaware of all this, all he cared about was that he didn't like any of them, and this was going to be a very long night.

The restaurant was arranged with circular tables each with four chairs, and so the gang sat together at two tables. 'How is you roommate?' said Baz to Rich.

'Nightmare, wanna swap?' he replied.

'No, I'm good,' said Baz.

'You're a real pal,' said Rich with a down at heel look on his face.

'Oh dear,' said BB 'Cheer up it may never happen.'

'Too late, it already has,' said Rich dismally.

Colin gave him a friendly tap on the arm 'I would swap Rich honest I would, but it's good to see you looking normal for a change without a silly grin on your face all the time, I think it will do you good.'

Rich scanned his friends faces as they all started to smile, his face broke into a smile too and then a laugh. 'This is a nightmare,' he said. 'I hope you know that you lot. But I suppose I'm a big boy now, so I will take this one for the team.'

'A regular hero,' said Steph. 'Sleeping with the enemy.'

They all laughed apart from Rach who was far more muted.

Dinner was actually quite good. There was a reasonable selection to choose from and they all ate heartily, not saying very much at all just concentrating on the job in hand.

Deirdre and Derek sat alone at a table nearby. They both had Cassoulet which was a French casserole with sausage and meat and beans in it. Both of them had fancied a glass of wine but decided against it in front of all the children and so they sipped the table water and chatted about the itinerary for tomorrow.

'Munich is another five-hour drive tomorrow,' said Derek. I'm pretty tired and I'm sure the kids are too. Why couldn't we have just flown to Munich?'

'I can't say for sure,' said Deirdre 'The Headmaster said it was too expensive, but I don't think it would have made much difference. I agree that the trip is longer, but it is such a rigmarole to fly nowadays, this is much easier and more fun too don't you think?'

'Well, someone has a short memory,' said Derek

'OK, except for the passport thing, I have enjoyed it so far,' rolling her eyes as she replied.

'Well, I for one will be glad when we get there,' said Derek.

'I'll drink to that,' said Deirdre as they both raised their glasses of water and continued with their meal.

'How's your room?' said Derek.

'I don't know, I haven't been to see it yet. I got the girls all organised and then came straight down here,' she said looking sheepish.

'You've had a sneaky glass of wine haven't you,' said Derek.

'This water is very refreshing don't you think?' said Deirdre with a twinkle in her eye.

'You crafty so and so,' said Derek then after a moment he added 'I wish I had thought of that.'

Deirdre smiled and continued eating.

After dinner it was getting pretty dark and due to the fact that they had an early start the next morning it was decided that they would all go straight up to their rooms.

'I don't want to see any boys on the first floor, or any girls on the second floor,' said Deirdre.

'Or teachers,' someone whispered behind their hand.

'What was that?' said Derek. Nobody spoke.

'Right off with you then,' he said as they got to the lifts and parted ways as they had done previously.

In their room V and Rach got ready for bed, and lay there chatting about the usual things they chatted about. The subject of boys never really came up as neither particularly wanted to go down that avenue just now. They were both beginning to realise that their friendship, although strong, was not necessarily going to be the biggest thing in their lives forever and other interests would, and were, coming along. It was a small elephant in the room, but they were both OK with that. When the time was right then they would talk about it.

Steph and BB sat on their beds. They had been friends a long time, and were as easy in each other's company as any two twelve-year-old girls could be. They were the doers and the thinkers in their little troupe. Two leaders could lead to conflict as one disagreed with another or felt undermined in some way as was the case with so many grown-ups, but not these two, they were like a left and right side of one brain, they moved together. The only fly in their ointment was a certain Richard Jenkins. Steph liked him, she tried to hide it, but you can't fool those closest to you. She knew Colin knew about it and she thought maybe BB knew too, but wasn't one hundred percent sure. She also knew that Rich had a soft spot for BB, and that was something that she was a little jealous about, and she didn't like the feeling of that jealousy, it felt dangerous, corrosive.

BB on the other hand was perfectly aware that Steph liked Rich, she liked him too, he made her laugh, but he was definitely not her type, and so in her mind they were only ever going to be just mates. She did know however that Colin and Steph were very close. They had been friends since before any of the rest of the gang had ever even met. They had a special bond of some kind that BB was intrigued about. It was like Steph didn't even notice that they had a deep connection either, why couldn't she see it? It was so obvious (to her anyway). She wished that she had that bond, she wished that she had that with Colin, (he was her secret crush). Nobody knew that of course and nobody ever would either.

Colin and Baz were chatting in their room,

'Poor old Rich,' said Colin.

'He'll live,' said Baz. 'He could sell sand to Arabia that boy, he'll always be OK that one.'

'That's true,' said Colin 'Still I've got a feeling something is brewing, don't ask me what or why or how, cos I don't know, but I've been thinking, and the thing is you and me Baz, we need to keep a vigil these next ten days. Look out for each other, you know,' he said.

Baz looked at his mate and saw the seriousness in his face. 'Does Rich know about this?' he said.

'No, he wouldn't take it seriously, and I don't want to worry the girls either. This is between me and you, right?'

'OK,' said Baz. He was pleased that Colin had confided in him above talking to Rich first, for once. He didn't know why or what it was about, but he was not going to let his friend down. 'Just between us then,' he said. Colin nodded and the subject was dropped.

Rich and Keith were in their room. Rich had put the tv on and was scrolling through the channels trying to find something to watch. 'Everything is in French,' he said. 'Even the football.'

'Leave that on and turn the sound down then,' said Keith.

Rich thought that was a good idea, so he grunted and did exactly that. The conversation was sparse and fairly monosyllabic. When the game had finished and as far as he could tell the blue team had beaten the white team by three goals to one, he turned the tv off and also his bedside light. He settled down into his covers to go to sleep. After a few moments he noticed that Keith was still wide awake. 'Turn your light off,' he said. 'Please.'

A few seconds later it went black and all he could see in the darkness was the red light on the tv. He could sense Keith was wide awake but perfectly still and quiet. He felt an energy coming from him, a nervous energy. He assumed it was just awkwardness and so eventually he drifted off to sleep.

Keith lay awake for a long time; he was glad to be away from home, but he kept his guard up at all times, even all this way away 'Jekyll and Hyde' he thought 'Jekyll and Hyde.' He wondered what his dad was doing right now. He wished he had his passport in his hand, but that was not possible. Miss Rhymer had put all the passports in the hotel safe overnight for safe keeping.

He missed his mum. 'Goodnight Mum,' he said in his head as he did every night.

Sometime later sleep came over him.

Derek and Deirdre had gone back downstairs and were sat at the bar.

'We can't stay here long,' said Deirdre. 'The girls might want me for some reason, so I had best go to my room.'

'I suppose you are right,' said Derek. 'Still, it's nice to have a quiet drink together again. This is the first time since..'

'No need to go over that again,' Deirdre cut in. 'We all say things we shouldn't,' she continued. At that precise moment she was actually thinking far more about her insensitivity towards Keith Henderson earlier that day than she was of Derek talking in the pub to a work colleague about their relationship. She had pretty much forgiven him straight away for that misdemeanour of course, but she wanted to make a point, and she had, but now she realised that he had suffered enough.

When they got back home she would make it up to him, but whilst they were on this trip, it was going to be strictly professional, it had to be. 'No inappropriate behaviour in Bavaria,' she thought to herself as she drained her glass and the said 'Shall we go?'

When they got to the lifts Derek said, 'Left or right?'

'Oh, I think we can chance a thirty second trip alone in a lift together Derek don't you?'

About ninety seconds later the lift opened on the second floor and two teachers exited with ruffled hair and smudged lipstick. One went along the corridor to his room while the other took the flight of stairs down to level one where she then went to check out her room for the first time.

By midnight everyone was sound asleep, the children, the teachers, even the driver too. Dreams were had. Some were random, some were not so random.

Colin slept badly, he tossed and turned, he even woke Baz up at one point in the night uttering words in his sleep.

At 6am all the rooms phones rang with a wakeup call.

Baz turned to Colin. 'You were having a dream, or some kind of nightmare last night,' he said.

'Was I?' said Colin.

'Yes, you were talking,' he replied.

'What did I say,' said Colin.

'To be honest I couldn't really make it out,' he replied. 'You said dad a few times and something about not worrying, then you said a word I didn't know, it sounded foreign, German maybe. I couldn't be sure.'

'What was the word?' said Colin.

'It sounded like Hutenghast, yes that's it Hutenghast.'

Even as he uttered the word it felt wrong coming out of his mouth and his hair stood on end. Colin felt much the same as he listened.

'Don't say it again,' he said. 'It's wrong, something is wrong about that word, something not good is coming, I can feel it. I have felt it for weeks now, this is what I was talking to you about earlier Baz. Something about this trip is off, not right. We need to be extra vigilant. Don't say anything to anyone about this. Though, we have to figure it out for ourselves, just me and you Baz, OK?'

He felt a little scared but even though the thought of his friends being in some sort of danger was bad enough, when he thought about V and everything that she had been through these last couple of weeks. Well, there was nothing that was going to frighten him enough to not protect her from harm, even if it was from something unspeakable.

'One hundred percent with you Col,' he said. 'Whatever it is, we got it, you and me, together.'

They shook hands, then they man hugged and went down to breakfast. The room was full, and they went over and sat with the others. Colin started a conversation as if nothing had passed between them.

'Sleep OK Rich?' said Colin

'Like a log,' he replied. 'Glad that's over, now let's get out of here and onto Bavaria and some fun.'

'Absolutely,' they all agreed.

Colin looked at Baz who returned the gaze, they both nodded just enough so that nobody else noticed.

They didn't know it of course but the game was already on, a game far darker than they could ever have imagined. At that precise moment it was just a feeling, originally it was Colin's feeling alone but now Baz felt it too.

Colin was glad, he realised that he and Baz were the foot soldiers here. Somehow they had to look out for and protect eighteen children and two teachers for a whole nine more days. It sounded stupid in his head, and he knew that it would sound even more ridiculous if it was shared with anybody else. Everyone would think that they had both lost the plot, nobody would listen, nobody would believe them, and so whatever this unspoken thing was that now felt so real, was not going to get whatever it was after, and nothing was going to get in their way of preventing this unknown thing from winning.

The Great Being was and ever had been, all knowing. The beast had had his cycle, now was the time for change. It was not the ordained way for him to intervene here himself, that was not how it was to be. No, change had to come from an unexpected source, and as he looked down at this scene below he felt that finally the time may have really come for this change. From this small group of men, women and children, one would hold the ultimate fate of The Hutenghast in their hand. When the time came, would they be able to take that chance? Others had tried in the past, and had failed, but things were different this time. The beast was weaker than ever before, his allies were few and his time was drawing near. Soon, very soon the change would come.

Chapter 22

After breakfast everyone got their things together and assembled in reception at the appointed time. The driver had brought the coach around from the parking area, and the children could see him stood beside it through the large reception windowed panels and revolving door. He was smoking a cigarette with a half-smile on his face just watching the scene inside. He could see that the male teacher, Derek, was looking rather self-important as usual while the lady teacher, Deirdre, was talking to the desk clerk about something. It looked like an argument of some kind about the passports as he could see that they both had passports in their hands, waving them around and clearly saying something to each about them. He had seen it all before and over the years he had learned to just observe, and say nothing.

The sooner he got to Munich and dropped them all off at the coach park, the quicker he could go on to Stuttgart to see his sister. He was not really a clock watcher type of person though, and so he continued to stand there watching on as if he hadn't a care in the world.

'No, you are wrong, there is one passport missing here!' Deirdre had been saying to the desk clerk.

'You have them all,' she had replied.

Deirdre sighed and looked at the girl. She was maybe nineteen or twenty and bore a striking resemblance to the hotel manager and so Deirdre assumed that this was indeed his daughter. 'Not much point calling him then,' she thought.

'Miss,' she said. 'I have twenty children here and only nineteen passports, so can you please look again in the safe to see if you misplaced the other one somehow, I gave you twenty two passports yesterday, mine and Mr Ford's passport are in my hand,' she said pointing towards Derek, 'there should be another twenty, one for each child, I have only nineteen here,' she repeated.

'What name is missing?' said the girl.

Deirdre thought this a stupid pointless question as there was either a passport in the safe, or there wasn't. She purposely hadn't spoken the name, as she did not want to worry the child in question unduly.

'What name?' the girl said again.

Reluctantly Deirdre replied 'Henderson, Keith Henderson.'

She looked around, the children giggled, all except Keith whose colour was draining from his cheeks as she looked at him.

'My passport!?' he squeaked.

'I'm sure it is in the safe, the desk clerk is going to check again now,' said Deirdre. She looked the girl in the eye and continued 'Aren't you?'

The girl sighed and bent down under the desk to look in the safe for a second time. All the passports had been put into a large envelope the evening before so there was no way one could simply jump out; she was thinking as she opened the door for a second time and examined the contents.

She was just about to stand up and say that there were no other passports in there when she noticed a dog eared and slightly worn-out passport at the back. She had seen it earlier and disregarded it as a relic, left there for some reason long ago. She picked it up and stood. She scanned the contents and read the name aloud, 'Ah Keith Henderson, yes apologies Madam, her it is.'

She handed the passport to Deirdre who said thank you through her teeth.

All the children saw the exchange, and also, more importantly, the state of Keith Henderson's passport.

'Blimey, it's the dead sea scrolls,' said Rich and the room erupted into laughter. Except it wasn't everybody, Keith Henderson and Rachel Stiles did not laugh. Rach looked across at his face, and realised this was more than utter embarrassment for him, there was far more there, this cut him very deeply, she could see that, so deeply in fact that tears were welling up in her eyes, and she fired back at the cacophony of noise.

'For goodness sake grow up you lot! Imagine if it was your passport that was missing, you wouldn't laugh then would you, you are all mean, I mean really mean!' she shouted.

Everyone was shocked and the laughter evaporated in an instant, in fact you could not hear a pin drop, the teachers, the desk clerk, her friends, the Dukes (who both stood there with their mouths open), and of course the boy himself all completely quiet. Keith Henderson's face was red, his eyes were bright with tears of relief, anger, humiliation and pain, all mixed together in one. He looked at Rach and then looked down at his shoes.

Rach felt an overwhelming urge to go over and give him a hug, but she restrained herself.

'Well anyway, it's not funny to laugh at others misfortune is it Miss, Sir?' she said looking at the teachers. 'Even if it is someone you may not get along with,' she continued. This was designed as a deflection (mostly for her friends benefit to avoid awkward questions coming her way). V of course smiled to herself, but said nothing.

'Yes, quite so Rachel,' said Deirdre once the moment had passed. 'All right drama over everyone, let's go, on the coach now,' she continued.

They all filed out.

Baz went over to V 'remind me not to ever get on her bad side,' he remarked.

'I think you're relatively safe,' replied V with a smile, 'I'll protect you, don't worry.'

They both blushed a little and boarded the coach for the last time.

Heads were counted. Derek and Deirdre sat down, and the coach moved off.

'What is it with passports this trip?' said Derek with a smirk.

Deirdre said nothing, she looked the other way so that he could not see her smiling. She was still annoyed a little at the desk clerk, but Keith Henderson's passport did indeed look like it had been around the world a dozen times, so the dead sea scrolls comment was quite amusing she had to admit. Keith himself on the other hand was sitting at the back, deep in thought. His insides were in turmoil, his feelings were all over the place. It took quite a while along the road to Munich before he was fully calm again and his walls came back up.

He was so glad that everyone was going their separate ways very soon, he could not keep up this Mr Hyde persona much longer. He was fed up with the Duke's and was privately extremely glad that he would be leaving them behind next year when they went to different schools. Of course, they had both served their purpose in his little charade, but now it was time to move on, and he was glad. Settling down in his seat, he looked out of the window at the passing countryside. The Duke's spoke to him a few times along the way, but he just grunted in reply, and so eventually they left him in peace.

Thoughts turned to his mum, and his dad. He contemplated all the changes that he would eventually make to his life. He was not going to be held back by anyone. He was not going to be responsible for anyone. The future for him was to be all about him, just him. His mum was gone, his father did not care, he was living an eternal lie and that was going to change.

'I'm not going to care about anyone, I'm not going to live like a shadow either,' he thought. 'It's going to be just me, just me. I deserve just me,' he thought to himself.

The intensity faded from his mind and his thoughts drifted to Rachel Stiles. This troubled him. He didn't want to feel anything for anyone, but he could not deny that she occupied his mind more and more, and that worried him, but it made him feel good too, all at the same time.

'I will be me, I will be free,' he thought.

Even as he was thinking this, deep down he knew that it was not certain, nothing ever was.

He had once thought that his mum would live forever, but he had been wrong about that. Was he wrong about this too?

It was a lot of baggage to carry for a boy of only twelve, but carry it he did. Even though it was in such a fractured and broken way.

Further up the coach V turned to Rach and whispered, 'That was a bit obvious Rach.'

'I just couldn't not say anything,' she whispered back. 'The look on his face, it was like his whole world was at stake or something, I can't explain it, but that passport means something more than just it's use to him as a passport,' she said. 'Anyway, it's done now, conversation over.'

'OK,' said V. 'We'll see.' She looked out of the window.

Colin turned to Rich, 'I know he is a twit, but I think Rach was right mate, that was a bit harsh back there.'

'Maybe,' said Rich, 'But do you think he would have kept schtum if it was you or me? Cos I don't.'

'Two wrongs don't make a right Richard,' said BB appearing through the gap between the headrests.

'Well, he's still a twit, and I don't like him,' replied Rich.

'That's not very grown up is it,' said Steph poking her head around the corner.

'OK, OK, I'm sorry,' said Rich.

'Are you going to apologise?' said BB.

'I think that is a step too far for Rich, BB,' said Colin

''You said it mate, he doesn't deserve an apology,' said Rich (even as he was saying it though he already knew that he was in the wrong here on two counts).

'I'll talk to him, OK? Sometime,' he said.

'Thank you Richard,' said BB.

Steph thought, 'He wouldn't do that for me!' It annoyed her.

Colin looked at BB 'You seem to have the ability to get everyone to do anything you ask,' he said in awe. 'I think you may well be Prime Minister or something one day, whatever you want to be you will be, I predict,' he said.

BB flushed a little at that. She smiled coyly and sat back in her seat. 'Ditto,' she said. 'I've seen the way you work Colin Hart; you point people in a direction you want them to go in too, and off they go.'

Colin looked at her, their eyes hovered for a second longer than would be the norm for them. BB looked away first.

Steph noted the look, and that bothered her too.

'What is wrong with me?' she thought to herself.

Chapter 23

The drive across the border into Germany went quickly enough, and without further issue. Nobody stopped the coach at the border, no-one wanted to look at passports or anything else, in fact it was seamless. You would never know that you were leaving France and entering Germany if it were not for a sign on the roadside stating the fact.

The coach skirted a place called Karlsruhe, and then headed off towards Stuttgart which was approximately halfway between Strasbourg and Munich.

The driver said very little as he drove, which was a blessing as far as Deirdre was concerned. He reminded her of a fly buzzing around that you can never catch. He always appeared to not pay any attention to what was going on conversationally on the coach, but she could tell that he was an antenna, listening into everything. This was why she always spoke to Derek in a whisper whilst they were travelling. That should have only been necessary if the coach had been sleek and quiet, but it wasn't in fact it was exactly the opposite. It was whiney and noisy, and it vibrated. Derek was constantly asking her to repeat what she had just said, or to speak up, and so by the time they got across the border and into Germany she had learned that it was better to say what needed to be said off the coach completely, and away from prying ears.

She looked at him as she was thinking all these things. He appeared harmless enough, friendly enough too in his quirky way, but whenever there were any issues, or a scene of some kind, there he was in the corner, across the foyer, outside by the coach, smirking, and shaking his head. He was always around.

'Oh yes mister,' she thought to herself. 'I know your game.'

'Excuse me Miss,' a voice said breaking her daydream.

Deirdre looked around to see Briony looking through the seat gap two rows behind her.

'Yes Briony, what is it,' she asked, a little annoyed at being distracted.

'Are we stopping for a short break soon?' she replied.

They had been on the road almost two hours and a break was due, so the question was reasonable enough.

'When we get past Stuttgart Briony, we will have a short rest break then, OK?'

'I know where to stops,' piped in the driver. 'Just off motorway in Stuttgart, nice park, nice café, very good,' he said.

He turned his head briefly and smiled at BB then carried on driving.

'Very well,' Deirdre replied, she couldn't exactly say no to something so innocuous.

'He orchestrated that!' she thought. 'The crafty little weasel must have asked Briony to say that, I bet anything his sister is at that café waiting when we get there.'

When they arrived at the park, which was indeed just off the main highway, the coach stopped in a bay near the cafe.

'OK back here in twenty-five minutes everyone,' said Derek as they all piled out.

Derek and Deirdre were last of all to get off, except for the driver. Deirdre wanted to linger and see where he was going to, but Derek said, 'Let's go see this park then, stretch our legs.'

Reluctantly she agreed and soon forgot about the whole incident. They had a very nice stroll around a small botanical garden with a lake. All the flowers were in bloom, which was quite beautiful to see, and to add to the scene it was turning out to be a rather lovely day too.

'Isn't this nice,' remarked Derek.

'Yes, very,' she replied.

As they walked back towards the coach they walked towards the café. Quite a few of the children were in there which was to be expected. 'Fizzy drinks and food are far more preferable at their age to a nice walk,' she thought. She was hoping that things would improve on their hikes through the Bavarian mountains. She was sure they would. There was something about mountains that was exciting, exhilarating. Her mind wandered, 'A little like steam trains,' she thought, 'They were exciting too, sort of alive like a living thing.'

Deirdre had been on a steam train as a small child, and there was just something about the smell, and all that noise, and the smoke, and the fire too. They were like a dragon.

'Look over there, the coach driver is chatting to a woman. They appear to be having a coffee together,' interjected Derek pointing at the café window as they approached.

Deirdre looked across and saw the coach driver sitting across a table from a woman that was so like him that it could only be..

'That must be his,' Derek started to say when Deirdre finished his sentence with the word 'Sister!'

'Crafty little,' Derek continued but was quickly cut off as Deirdre once again completed his sentence. 'Weasel!' she said

'I was going to say Super Mario, that's who he reminds me of,' continued Derek.

'Yes, I suppose he does look a little like him,' said Deirdre. 'But he acts like a weasel.'

'Bit strong, but I admit he's a crafty one, I think all coach drivers are like that. Part of the job description I'll bet,' said Derek with a grin.

She looked at him and broke into a smile, and then a laugh.

'C'mon,' she said, 'Let's get back to the coach before he sees us looking at him.'

Off they went. As they passed the window the driver looked across and smiled.

'He's a funny one that driver,' BB mused from inside the café as she sat there eating the croissants and drinks with Steph that he had bought for them. 'Shame he's not coming all the way with us.'

Steph wasn't really listening, but she grunted a response. She had been wondering what was up with Colin and Baz. They were huddled together in the corner of the café on their own, without Rich too which was odd in itself. They looked concerned, worried even. She wanted to know what was going on, but something told her to leave them alone. 'I hope everything is alright with Colin,' she thought. 'It must be, otherwise he would have told me, he always confides in me,' she thought. 'Always has and always will, I guess.' She didn't mind, never had done.

They had known each other like forever and although she had never really thought about it much before, losing touch with Colin was not really an option. They were just too close, and that was that. She had thought of their relationship as reliable friends, nothing more, until now, maybe.

Chapter 24

When everyone was safely back on the coach they headed southeast again on the road to Munich. The gang had moved seats, and the girls were now together on one side with the boys on the other.

BB was going through the itinerary with the girls, while the boys were just chatting about this and that.

Baz was thinking. He had wanted to talk to Rich about the problems that may or may not be ahead as soon as he had found out about it all himself, but Colin was adamant they should keep it quiet and had said a firm 'No'. He had been quite forceful about it.

'He's great Rich.' Colin had said. 'We can rely on him if things get rough later on, but telling him now? I am not sure that is the best idea, but he mustn't know that, as it would upset him. If we told him this now he would just take the mickey, or blab to the girls maybe. I might be out of line here and he would be fine. I thought about telling him Baz, you know when I told you,' he had continued, 'But you know what a joker he is. I didn't want to take any risks.'

Baz had agreed that it made sense, but he still didn't like the thought of hiding anything from the gang, even the girls. They were just as capable and formidable as the boys in a tight spot, even more so probably. But this was Colin's call, it was his warning, or his dad's and that meant that he was always going to go along with what he said 100%.

BB got out her notepad upon which she had worked out what was going to happen on the whole trip. They had been given a rough outline by the school of course, but her notes were much more extensively detailed.

'Well girls, from Munich we travel to Garmisch Partenkirchen. It's a ski resort in the winter so lots of mountains around, in fact it is near Germany's highest peak, which is called Zugspitze, it is nearly three thousand metres high so will have snow on the top all year round,' she explained. 'We were apparently supposed to be staying in Garmisch itself, but at the last minute we had to divert to alternative accommodation,' she continued.

'Why is that?' said Steph.

'I'm not entirely sure, but I overheard that the Headmaster had some weird call from some lady in the resort. There had been a mix up, a double booking or something. Anyway, alternative arrangements had been made for us all to stay in some big fancy house halfway up a mountain nearby called Alpspitze. It turns out that it is nearer to most of the places we are going to walk through anyway, like Lake Eibsee, and so it was agreed that we would stay there instead, even though it is kind of remote. Sounds like fun eh?'

'You don't miss much do you,' said V.

BB smiled, 'Just taking note, that's all, always be prepared I say.'

Colin had overheard this, and little alarm bells were ringing in his head. 'Last minute changes are not a good thing,' he thought.

He looked at Baz and realised that he had also been listening to BB too. Did this have anything to do with the misgivings he had? Anything was possible.

BB went through the whole thing with the girls while Colin and Baz listened on. Their guide was to meet them at the accommodation, and the next coach was dropping them near Lake Eibsee. They had to walk from there which was about 4 miles.

'Miss has the map, she knows where to go,' said BB. 'I think it's exciting, just trekking with a map into the mountains.'

Some of the girls looked quite keen, others were not so enthralled by the prospect. Colin definitely wasn't happy, the hairs twitched on the back of his neck.

Mid-morning, they hit the light traffic on the outskirts of Munich, the bus station was right in the centre of the city, so it took about twenty minutes to get there. The children were all fascinated by the scene, lots of modern buildings sitting alongside grand buildings, palaces and gardens, it was beautiful. Everything seemed to run like clockwork too, and everywhere you looked it was clean.

The coach rolled up at the bus station and stopped in one of the bays there. The bus station was right next to the central train station. In truth it was just a large transport hub, efficient and organized.

'Finally, we can get off this coach and actually enjoy this trip now away from that awful little man,' Deirdre thought as she watched the driver unloading everybody's rucksacks from the bowels of the coach. He looked as happy about it as she did, which irked her a little, but she put that to the back of her mind as everyone collected their things and said their farewells to the weasel. She grunted at him as he said to her 'Enjoy your trips, I will be here in nine days' time, same place OK?'

'Thank you,' said Derek handing him their contact details just in case.

The transport that was to take them to Garmisch had also been diverted and the new instructions had been to wait where they were for pickup which would then take them to the new destination at Lake Eibsee. The teachers didn't seem perturbed by this at all, neither did the rest of the children, it was all part of the adventure. Only Colin and Baz were thinking this was all very odd, kind of weird. Steph didn't think this anything out of the ordinary particularly either, but she had continued to observe Colin and Baz, and she was still a little unsettled, she was tempted to confront them about it, but she didn't.

Chapter 25

Margaret was so pleased with her little plan. It had been so easy to find out what the school had chosen to do. When she realised that the brochures had done the trick, she set to work. She had found out where the children were to stay, where they intended to go whilst they were there, in fact everything that she needed to know, in order to plan how to get them to her house at the right time. Once her plan was set, she had contacted the headmaster and re-arranged everything. She had been so plausible on the phone that he hadn't even bothered to check if what she had told him was accurate. 'Fool,' she had thought. 'Oh well done, you fool.'

She could feel them closer now, so close. She knew they had arrived in Munich and were awaiting the onward transport that she had arranged. It was unfortunate that her current home was too remote for them to be brought directly to her door, but that was too contrived, too obvious anyway. She did not want to arouse any suspicion, it was true that the road was too narrow and winding, and only tractors or four-wheel drive vehicles could scale the track, even in summer, and so rather than risk them all falling to their deaths in a ravine, which would have served no purpose at all, she had concluded that a small trek was low risk for a great reward. They would happily walk into her trap, find the telling, read it and be damned.

The Hutenghast, had allowed Margaret to make all the necessary arrangements this time, he saw what she always did, her contrivances pleased him, but and he also felt the nearness, the presence of the seven, and it had clouded his judgement.

She would not fail him, she could not fail him, he had thought. The alternative for her was a fate far, far worse than Emily's fate. She had merely returned to the dust from whence she had come when it was her time. Her task completed.

No, failure for Margaret (who still had much to do in his service), would be eternal, it would be dark, and it would be utterly hopeless.

He was weaker now, conserving his strength was the key to survival, and so he was, without realising it, fully allowing fate to intervene for the very first time. Certainty in all things had been all too absorbing of his power since his other servants had failed and fallen by the wayside, and so had taken a risk, he had no other option.

Margaret was completely unaware of his precarious predicament, and that was how he intended it should remain. She thought of him as an all-powerful being, impossible to resist, but he was far from that right now. He was vulnerable, and that was a thing that struck him with great fear, but also great resolve.

Far above The Great Being, who saw all things, but who would never directly interfere, could see beyond the present time. He could foretell what was possible, not necessarily what would come to pass, rather what could come to pass. The situation was tenuous for the beast now, he could see that, he knew of the failures, he could see his reliance on mortals. That could be his downfall, he thought. He would therefore continue to observe, the situation was turning towards the good and that pleased him. Not long now, he thought, not long.

Chapter 26

The children and the teachers watched the coach depart in a puff of black smoke and almost before the smog of it had dissipated a very old bus came into view, it drew alongside, and it stopped in the very spot Super Mario's coach had just inhabited. It was very old and out of place compared to the other modern coaches and buses. Super Mario's coach looked a little decrepit, but this thing was positively archaic, it looked like a movie prop, but weirdly it had made barely a sound.

The door opened and a driver stepped out. Derek had expected to see a usual coach driver, burly, a little overweight from too much sitting down, too much eating, not enough exercise (much like himself), but he was surprised to see a man, neatly dressed and in a dark suit. He looked directly at Deirdre and picked up her bag. He had a blank face which was 'unremarkably plain' she thought.

Derek was thinking much the same as Deirdre was, and was just about to speak to him when he said, 'This way Ma'am, Sir, children, best be on our way.'

Without waiting for a reply of any kind he walked off with her bag in his hand towards the rear of the old bus, he opened up a compartment, and started putting all the baggage in.

'Here we go again,' said Rich. 'The next coach will probably be drawn by a horse.'

The driver gave Rich an even look which was completely lost on him.

'Oh well,' said Deirdre. 'Everybody get on board, I can see the driver is eager to be off, as are we all.' She climbed up and got into a seat just behind the driver's seat. It was remarkably comfortable, and the inside felt much more spacious than it had appeared from the outside. The children all filed in and found places to sit, Derek sat next to Deirdre. The driver climbed into his seat, and closed the doors with a lever of some kind, there were no electronics on this bus.

Derek did a head count; everyone was accounted for. As he sat back in his seat two things struck him, firstly the head height was vast, he hadn't needed to stoop at all as he walked up and down counting heads, the second thing was he realised every seat was occupied, not a single spare space, this bus had twenty-three seats on it and no more.

Everyone felt the movement as the bus took off, but it was completely silent and utterly smooth, belying its external appearance.

'Is this thing electric?' said Baz.

'I don't know mate,' said Colin, 'but it is..'

'Odd?' interjected Rich.

'Yes, that is one way of putting it,' he replied. 'Don't worry Dad,' he thought. 'I'm on the case, me and Baz and Rich, just like you and your mates, the Three Amigos, eh Dad.' He smiled a nervous smile to Baz, and resolved to fill Rich in as soon as they got off this silent and eerie bus.

As they drew out of the station the bus went through a large puddle of water by the side of the road, as it drove away no wet tracks could be seen behind it. It was just like it had never even been there at all.

Chapter 27

The journey from Munich to Lake Eibsee was a little surreal for Colin and Baz. Maybe their senses were heightened more now, all the last-minute changes to the planned schedule was a massive red flag for both of them. Was something, or someone interfering here with their trip in any way? The gang had been discussing this Bavaria trip for about a year, the norm for their school was for the destination to be somewhere that didn't require a passport, like the Isle of Wight, or Snowdonia, or the Peak District, somewhere like that. Everybody had agreed that even if it was to be camping in the headmaster's back garden, then they were all up for it, whatever. When they found out that they were actually going abroad, it had been excitement ramped up to eleven.

'Oh wow, this is crazy!' V had said to Rach when she was given the news.

It had been, as always, in the form of a letter from the school, very formally written, almost like an invitation to a fancy party or something, but that didn't matter, the message was clear, the school trip was abroad, abroad! How fantastic was that?

Steph and BB had both travelled extensively with their parents many times and so they were a little more 'feet planted on the ground' about it all. Yes, it was great, and a much better option than going to the Cotswolds or something, but the main thing for them was just everyone being together, on a trip, one last hurrah.

Colin, Rich and Baz were all very cool about the whole thing to each other, at least on the surface, but inside they were, all three of them, as excited as a small child opening their presents under the tree on Christmas morning.

'Oh yeah, Bavaria, that's Germany, right?' Rich had said. 'Some good football teams in Germany, I wonder if we will get to go and see a match,' he continued.

'I don't think the girls would think that was very fair, do you?' said Colin. 'We would probably have to go watch a netball match too or something.'

'Do they play netball in Germany?' said Rich.

'Yes,' said Baz, 'I saw them play Great Britain in the Olympics once.'

'Who won?' said Rich.

'We did,' said Baz.

'That makes a change then,' Colin had said. 'We rarely win a football match against them do we?'

'I suppose not,' mused Rich. 'Still Germany eh? It beats me how the headmaster went for it, abroad and all that, but I'm game (no pun intended),' he had concluded.

The other boys and girls were all mostly keen to go too, but some could not for varying reasons. And so it was that twenty of the thirty-one pupils from form 4C were signed up, and that had been just enough to make the trip viable.

The tortured boy was also one of the twenty to be going. In case you hadn't already guessed, the boy is of course, Keith Henderson.

Keith's mum was long gone, and his dad was well and truly off the rails. He realised that his dad was probably just as lost as he was. His life was a misery, some of it of his own making of course. To an outsider, what he had done to protect himself would have been an understandable defence mechanism. Adults put barriers up, tell lies, behave in a way that is different to how they really feel inside. Sometimes it is to just cope, or to fit in, be popular, or to try to be attractive to an employer, or a person of the opposite sex too. There were many reasons. But for Keith, it was entirely different. He didn't want to fit in, or be noticed. His lie was the opposite of that. He did not want to be noticed, or to fit anywhere. No, he wanted no questions, he wanted no one to bother him. It was to be just him and his predicament, working it all out alone.

Alone that was until Rachel Styles had come flying into his orbit, she made him think in a different way, a scary way. He had been so far down a hole that it had felt pointless to try and climb out of it. That was what he had thought these last couple of years, and so, as a consequence, he had become more morose, more difficult, more unpopular. He used to like it that way. It was a masochistic thing, but now he felt…different.

He looked around at the other children as they travelled along the road towards Lake Eibsee that day. There wasn't a single boy or girl aboard that he could consider a friend. Yes, he hung around with the Duke twins, but they were nasty through and through, he knew that, and it had dragged him down to their level. Nobody saw what was going on here, not the teachers, not the other children, not his dad, nobody. He had been a boy drowning for a long time, too long, awaiting the day when he could grow up and change his life.

He had worked so hard this last year at school, unnoticed by everyone, to get into the boy's grammar school. That was going to be the fresh start. He was going to leave behind his childhood in the embers of a final school trip and then, like a phoenix, he would be reborn next year.

That was how it played out in his head anyway. It was a childish scenario, from the thoughts of a child who was in chaos, but had Rachel come along as a lifeline? He had pondered over this. He had also considered that it would be very difficult next year, with Colin Hart and the other boys from junior school. They were going to all be at the grammar together. When he turned up there and started acting differently, they would all think he was being fake instead of actually trying to be real for the first time in three years.

He had decided that he could live with their derision. Maybe one day they could even be civil to each other again, if not friends, then at least not enemies. He was sick of enemies.

Then one day, not long ago, Rachel had looked at him and he had looked at her. Something had passed between them in that first look, it was like the chains and shackles that he had forged for himself, were now mere paper chains that could be cast aside at a moment's notice. But he was scared and so he waited, he avoided her, even though he longed for change, it would have to wait. Rachel would have to wait, he wasn't ready to leave his self-imposed chrysalis, not just yet.

Chapter 28

In the beginning Mr Hart knew nothing. Over time he realised that when he was awake he was not really 'awake' at all. He was, in actual fact, in some perpetual state of a kind where all words were lost to him. He could not understand, he was unable to open his eyes, move his limbs, or open his mouth to speak. He was in a veritable straight jacket. At first he was a little agitated but relatively unconcerned, his thoughts were rambling, and his mind had been damaged from the event that had put him in this position. As more time elapsed he became aware of his surroundings a little more day by day. He was in a hospital, so he was actually still alive, which did come as a shock to him as he had thought up to that point (after he was able to reason again) that he was between worlds, in some transient state moving towards whatever we humans go to when our earthly lives have passed. The realisation that he was not in fact dead had seemed to boost his resolve, and as a result the recovery of his senses. After a time, he could recognise the voices of the hospital staff, remember their names from the conversations that they had over his bed discussing his trauma and his condition. He still couldn't quite understand what it all meant but he knew that they were helping him and that was a comfort in some way. His family were gone in his mind at the start of this, he didn't even know his own name but now he could recognise his wife's voice and his son's too, he remembered them. They were talking to him gently, asking him questions, stroking his forehead and holding his hand. If only he could open his eyes to look into their faces and move his lips and speak. He would tell them of the joy they brought into the room when they came to visit him.

Slowly but surely his memories were returning. His mind was repairing itself. He spent many hours working on his thoughts and his memories as he lay there. He was exercising his brain, and as he did so everything slowly came back. He realised that his mates were there sometimes too, their friendship meant so much to him. Everybody meant so much to him.

This state of inertia was something that he had to overcome; he knew that. Now he was getting stronger each passing day, although time was not a concept he could really put into a category anymore. Everything was constant and unchanging physically, but mentally he was moving forwards, ever forwards.

And then just as his mind was returning to him, the beast came.

It had been lurking in the shadows during the times when he was not in control of his thoughts, when he understood nothing, he realised nothing. This was during 'sleep' he had recognised that. Yes, although he was completely inert and his eyes were always closed, he had times of sleep and periods of being awake also. It was so weird, and also frustrating, but he could do nothing to control it or change anything in any way.

The first time he realised the presence of another being in his lonely world was just after his wife and son had been to visit him. Normally his wife spoke far more than his son did (he could not remember Colin's name at this point). But on this day his son had been quite animated, words were still mostly a mystery to him, but snippets here and there struck a chord, and he realised that his son was telling him that he was going somewhere and soon. He recognised enough to realise that it was something to do with friends. He had been on a trip with his best friends when they were young lads and so he was glad for him, he wanted to say something or give him something, but all he could do was listen.

After they had left him that day, and after the night came, (he could tell when night arrived as the warmth of the sun was no longer on his face and the temperature fell), plus all the noises abated. The beep of the machine that he was plugged into was the only noise he heard at night. Beep, beep, beep. He drifted off, and he heard the noise no longer.

A movement in the recesses of his mind made him pick up with a start. It wasn't a dream he was experiencing here; this was different. Something had actually entered his mind. He was not sure what it was, but it was there, watching him. Occasionally it moved, or so he thought but it was so difficult to tell. It was like when you catch movement in the corner of your eye, you look towards it as quickly as you can, but nothing is there, although you know for certain that something was there just a moment ago. This something or someone was watching, and it unsettled him. Because it was not a good something, it was a bad someone, and he realised even then the very first time that it appeared, that no good would come from its presence.

Chapter 29

The bus driver knew his task, it was to transport the party to Lake Eibsee. He was not to divert in any way from this task. He was not to be distracted or delayed in any way; Margaret had been very direct in her instructions to him about that. He was intimidated by her, she was different to the others, the ones that had come before. She was decisive, her gaze was like the beast itself when she was angry. He felt she was 'like him', and so he was wary, careful. The others had all been trapped, they were as much victims as the chosen ones, but her, this Margaret, she was different, and he knew better than to disobey.

The beast himself (yes he knew the name but was forbade to say it, or to even think it) had come to him in a dream long ago. His longevity and his good fortune were a direct consequence of his acquiescence to the instructions of the beast.

He was just as caught up in this grisly affair as Margaret was, as they had all been, but it seemed to him that as a faithful foot soldier he had received all the benefits without the risk. His task was a simple one, to facilitate, to provide transportation, that was it, nothing more. Get them to where they were to be taken and then leave. He could go and live a normal life again until he was called upon once more.

He was fully aware that people were to be sacrifices to a greater cause, and even though in this case it was children he still felt that no blood was on his hands. He did his part, and when the deed was done, he himself also had new vigour. Not rebirth like the women, he never really aged at all, he just stayed the same. It was a fact that the beast needed him as much as he did the old women, he was just as important, but in his delusion he thought that he was not as culpable. Only time would tell if this was so. He drove on.

Deirdre looked at the driver and turned to Derek. 'Do you know what?' she said. 'It pains me to say this, but I think we would have been better to stay with the weasel until we got to the lake. Why did we need to change in Munich? Couldn't he have taken us all the way? After all it is only about eighty miles more, so why did we change?'

'I didn't like to question the headmaster about it too much,' said Derek. 'He mentioned something about arrangements had been made by the hotel and it was all at no cost to the school. When he spoke to Watts Coaches about it they were more than happy as the designated driver was staying in Stuttgart anyway, so it made sense, I guess.'

'He's odd,' she said. 'Look at him, his face is completely blank, he doesn't say a word, hasn't looked round once, he just drives.'

'That is his job,' said Derek.

'Yes, but, I think he's weird, and so is this bus it's like the Tardis, small on the outside, huge inside, and it's so quiet,' Deirdre went on.

'Well that old coach from Watts was like having an eight-hour massage as far as I was concerned, and not in a good way either, so I am good with it being nice and quiet thank you very much. Stop worrying about it Deirdre, we are almost there now anyway. This is the last leg and then it's just walking, us and the kids. No coaches, no buses, no weasels, no..'

Deirdre cut him off 'Alright, I get it, I am worrying about nothing, I know,' she said still unconvinced.

''That's right let's just enjoy this trip, we can make it a great experience for the kids. Don't tell anyone but I'm going to miss this bunch next year.'

'Me too,' said Deirdre, 'Me too.'

She looked out of the window and said no more.

'I have never been on anything so quiet,' Rich said to Baz and Colin. 'This bus is really cool, it must be electric or something even though it's old, maybe it was converted. And it's weird too, you get no feeling of moving really but when you look out the window we are travelling pretty quickly. And have you noticed the traffic? There are loads of vehicles out there, but nobody seems to get in our way, we haven't stopped once yet. Not at a junction, traffic lights, nowhere. We just keep going along, silently.'

Colin looked at Baz and they nodded in unison.

'Listen mate,' Colin said to Rich. 'There is something that we need to tell you. Don't laugh, don't interrupt either because this is serious and you need to be up to speed, OK. We need you with us on this, you can't tell anyone, the girls, the teachers, nobody, OK? This is our problem, well my problem, but anyway I need you both on board with me, I need you,' he said looking at Baz as he spoke.

Rich never looked serious, well not very often anyway, but his face hardened as he listened, he could see how earnest his friends were.

'So, this was something between you and Baz and now you decide to tell me. Is that it?' he said.

'No, not exactly,' said Colin, 'It's just that we shared a room last night and I was talking in my sleep, and it just came out that's all.'

'What came out.'

'That's what I am about to tell you,' said Colin 'This isn't personal, or about favouritism or anything stupid like that, this is serious OK so listen up.'

The boys huddled together, and Colin went over the whole story about his dad and the dreams and the strange things that were happening. The school trip, the change of plans, this bus, everything was leading towards something, something unexpected.

Rich listened as they spoke, and when they had told him everything he paused. After a few moments he said, 'So this, whatever it is, is what exactly?'

'That's just it, we don't know,' said Baz. 'But we have to protect the girls right?'

'Right!' they replied together. Colin was thinking about Steph, Baz about V and Rich realised that he was thinking about BB. He liked her a lot he realised. Well, he already knew that he liked her a lot, but this thought of some unknown danger had merely brought that feeling into much sharper focus.

'Why can't we tell Mr Ford though?' said Rich.

'Can't risk it, not yet,' said Colin. 'But if, or when the time comes, he will be the first to know. As it stands it's just gut feelings and dreams, right? Nobody will take that too seriously will they?'

'Well in that case I think that you have just sold it to me mate,' said Rich as the bus sped on its totally uninterrupted way towards its final destination.

Across the aisle the girls were chatting. Rach looked at the other three girls and said, 'What are those three being so secretive about, all bunched together and whispering.' As she looked across at the boys.

'Probably something banal,' said BB.

'Or stupid,' said V.

'It's the same thing,' said BB. 'What do you think?' she said to Steph.

Steph had been watching the boys. Whatever was going on, that was definitely what they were now talking about she was pretty sure about that, but Colin hadn't confided in her about it yet. Lots of people whose close friends haven't shared a secret with them, but had already told others would have been offended by now, but not Steph. She knew that Colin would talk to her about whatever it was, as soon as he thought it was right to do so, and she was going to respect that even though she was indeed a little miffed, as she was entitled to be.

'I think they are moaning about Keith Henderson being at grammar school next year with them,' she lied. Although it was pretty certain that they weren't too thrilled about that prospect.

'At least Tweedle Dum and Tweedle Dee won't be there with him to back him up all the time I suppose,' said BB. 'Those two are trouble.'

Rach bristled. 'He deserves to go, he passed didn't he? Why is everyone down on him all the time. I don't think he's so bad.'

'Oh really,' said Steph snapping out of her thoughts on Colin's dilemma. 'That's very interesting, would you care to elaborate?'

Rach reddened and then V came to her rescue.

'Come on girls,' she said. 'No cat fights, have you three already forgotten that I was going to be at a different school to you, my best friends! Only last week things were hopeless, and now they're not. So, I think Rach is right to defend someone who has passed the exam, you all earned your place, and you deserve to go, so he does too right? And so do I.'

'Well since you put it that way, then yes,' said Steph. 'Sorry.'

'Friends?' said BB

'Friends,' they all chimed in reply.

Chapter 30

Margaret was sleeping and awaiting instructions. The Hutenghast often came to her as she slept, especially when the time was close to 'The Refreshing.' She had never seen the beast in the form of actual flesh, but she knew that he could take that form should he so wish, but in her unconscious state she did see him. She was not sure if the thing before her was just her imagination, or this was indeed how he really was, or how he really sounded when he spoke to her.

The first time he came to her, he lurked in the shadows a while and then there he was talking to her. The voice was deep and powerful, it was enticing. It embraced all the words as it spoke, and she was intoxicated by it. Gradually he moved towards her until she could see what manner of being it was that spoke this way. She should have been scared stiff, terrified out of her wits, but she had already signed her pact with him, there was no going back now, so what point was there in being scared of his appearance.

She was becoming a much stronger woman than she had ever thought possible of herself, and that was mesmerising for her too. It was, in fact, all-encompassing, and so when the Hutenghast finally revealed himself, she was not afraid, merely exhilarated, she was on a journey few had ever been on, and few more would ever take.

The sacrificial ones would see him in a different way to her as he took them of course, but to her he was simply magnificent. He was tall. His arms and legs were impossibly long in comparison to his lithe body, he was like a spider in a way. His body, arms and legs were all covered in hair that was dark and matted but it seemed to glisten and shine even in the dark. His feet and his hands were devoid of hair, and they too were long and bony, dark claws and nails extended from each digit. His face was human like, but elongated too, his nose was almost like the snout of a bear but with thick lips at the end of it. She had expected his teeth to be pointed and yellow, but they were much as a man's teeth were, except that they were all incisor teeth as far as she could see. His ears were wolf like and pointed with long tufts of hair protruding from the top. His eyes were deep, deep blue, almost black so dark blue in fact that you could not discern what was pupil and what was iris. The whites of his eyes were only visible if he opened them very wide or looked from side to side, but when she saw them they were not white at all, they were only red. A dark blood red and they flickered like a flame. Yes, his eyes were like fire but in contrast to this, when he spoke it was as if there was a hoar frost coming from his mouth, for everything in the path of his breath turned a feathery white with frost.

He was hot and he was cold, and she was in total awe of him.

As she slept on this particular day, he came to her she as expected. She noticed that his demeanour, and his look was different to what she had become to expect from all their previous encounters. She couldn't put a finger on exactly what was different. It was true that his voice was edgier today, but she put that down to eagerness, the time was close after all. But no, it wasn't that, it was something else. She looked him over discretely trying not to stare for too long. Staring was something that could be very incendiary, she knew that, and so she darted her eyes to and fro so that he would not notice her unusual attention. There is something, she thought. It definitely wasn't his body, or his face as they appeared to be exactly as they always were.

Then he caught her looking. 'What ails you woman,' he said 'Do I sense hesitation? Are you hesitant Margaret, are you?' he continued as his voice rose.

'No, no I am as excited as you master,' she said.

'Don't lie to me!' he roared, his eyes rolled, and then she saw what it was that was different about him. The red was gone from his eyes, they no longer flickered like a flame, they were grey and lifeless, like a dead fish. All his power seemed diminished then. He sensed that she could feel this weakness and his tone changed. Menacingly he approached her as she slept, his mouth opened, and the coldness began to engulf her. She knew that this was what he did to the chosen ones, and she became rigid with fear.

'I could take your soul Margaret, right now if I so wished,' he said. 'Except that you no longer have a soul do you. Your soul is already mine. You sold it to me as a trinket for me to play with as I see fit. You can be as dust any time I wish, or you can be raised up, special,' he continued. 'I own you Margaret, do not fail me,' he roared.

'I will not master,' she said. Then he left her.

She awoke and thought on what she had just witnessed, an unease came over her, her skin went icy cold. She had been confident `before her nap, so confident about what was to come to pass over the next few days, but now? Now she felt something that she had not felt for a very long time, she felt mortal, she felt uneasy. She thought of the way that The Hutenghast had been with her. He was weaker, there was no doubt of that, she did not know why this was so, as she had never seen him in any other way than she had always seen him, strong, powerful, perfect. But now, the fire in his eyes was gone, he looked vulnerable, and that was something entirely new to her, and from what she could tell, it was new to him also.

This Refreshing had to be precise, there could be no hiccups, nothing could go awry. The driver was close to the drop off point now, so what could happen? Nothing, she thought, nothing will happen, nothing will go wrong.

Far above the Great Being, who saw all things, looked down on Margaret, she used to know him, but she was lost now and that caused him discomfort. He blamed the Hutenghast for her predicament, and for all the countless others who had fallen under his sway since the start of time. But today Margaret was not his main concern. The travellers were close now, the driver would not fail without his intervention and that was something that he could not, he would not do. Fate had to play its part here but the time for him to take some steps was here now surely. The Hutenghast was closer to defeat than ever before, but he could not wield the sword himself or deal the fatal blow, that was to be another. What he could do though was to control the heavens and the earth as he had always done, and so he looked down again at Margaret, and at the driver, and at the passengers and he was content.

Wheels could be set in motion; something could be done. Fate and good fortune were at play here against manipulation and deceit. Which would survive? So often it had been the latter, but now he hoped that finally this time things may be different, they needed to be different.

And who was to be the one to make a difference here?

Of the twenty-two on the bus only one would come forward, this was always going to be the way. Since the start of time the Great Being had known that those cast down would ultimately fail, and one by one this had come to pass until the present day when only the beast called Hutenghast, plus one other, who was lost to this world, were left. He was alone now save for his servants who cared not for him, but only themselves. All the other dark being,s that worried The Earth had been defeated by one, the Great Being had made no interventions in these defeats in times past, but now was different, this was the final piece. He realised that he and the Hutenghast were like two pieces on a chessboard, one black, one white, one move left on each part. Make your move Hutenghast he thought, let us see what will transpire, beast.

The bus approached the stop point at Lake Eibsee and the driver slowed to a stop. 'Here we are,' was all that he said as he got up from his seat and exited onto the tarmac, opened the hatch at the rear of the bus and put the contents onto the kerbside. By the time he had finished this all the children and the teachers were there beside him watching as the last bag hit the floor. He went into his pocket and pulled out a map which he handed to Derek.

Opening it up Derek could see it was a map of the lake and the mountains and passes all around. A meandering red line had been drawn on the map from the position they were at next to the lake, it went up into the foothills and mountains beyond. It appeared to veer off the designated walkways, but this was clearly the way they were to go to get to their accommodation.

'Follow the red line,' said the driver pointing off into the distance towards the mountains.

'But this goes off the trail,' said Derek.

'You won't go wrong Sir,' he said. 'Just follow the red line.'

Derek wanted to quiz him once more, but as he turned around again the driver had walked away, in fact he was already in the bus. Almost silently he drove away and the twenty-two were left there standing alone together.

'Oh well children,' said Derek. 'Looks like we are on our own now so pick up your gear and let's go, er this way,' he said holding the map and pointing in the same direction that the driver had.

The gang all looked at each other. Colin smiled at Steph, 'Come on then,' he said, 'The fun starts here.'

Off they went in a straight line towards the mountains and their destiny.

Part III

Chapter 31

Derek held the map out in front of him, to any bystander he would look utterly confident, portraying an aura that he knew exactly where he was going, but in actual fact, inside he was only half convinced of that. He could follow a guided trail just like anybody else, could but this one veered off halfway up the mountain to goodness knows where and he was a little insecure about that, but he was not going to let on about his insecurities to Deirdre or the children. He was going to bluff it out, after all the driver had said 'You can't go wrong as long as you follow the red line,' and so they couldn't. Could they? He brushed aside that thought and marched on with Deirdre and the children in tow. After a while they caught a glimpse of the lake below as they climbed up into the foothills. The late afternoon sun glistened across the water's surface, shimmering and dancing in the eyes of the observers.

'Beautiful isn't it,' said Deirdre next to him.

Everyone looked down at the view and a few 'yes Miss's' were heard.

'We must walk around it while we are here,' she continued. 'Don't you agree Mr Ford?' she said to Derek.

'Derek?' she said a little louder.

'Er yes dear, I mean Miss Rhymer,' he spouted as he realised that she was addressing him. The children sniggered and Deirdre looked at him in a less than pleased manner.

'Something wrong?' she said.

'No, no everything is fine. We should get there well before the sun goes down as long as we keep going and don't dawdle too much,' he replied.

Deirdre's face didn't show any signs of an improved demeanour as they continued upwards, she was a little annoyed to say the least that the trip was unnecessarily complicated, at least in her view anyway. She had not been aware of the late changes to arrangements and that needled her to start with but now they were following a map that had a rough trail drawn on it in red biro. Worse still it was given to them by some weird bus driver who just told them to follow it, and everything would be fine. Well, they were following it, and everything wasn't fine. She felt a little uneasy with it all and so, as far as she was concerned, the blame for this little unfolding fiasco lay with Derek Baden Powell and this silly map.

She was looking at Derek as she thought all this. She liked Derek, a lot, but he could be, well, very annoying at times, and right at this moment she was annoyed with him, but she did not want to alert the children to any friction so she gritted her teeth. She smiled falsely, and she carried on walking up the slope of the trail and away from the lake, away from any decent phone signal, and off towards whatever they were supposed to find when they got to wherever they were supposed to be going. She continued to fume silently as they walked on, and the sun gradually sank lower and lower in the sky.

The trio (Colin, Baz and Rich) looked at each other. 'It's starting,' Colin whispered to the other two. 'Can you feel it?' They both nodded. For the first time since being informed of the concerns that the other two had, Rich felt truly uneasy. Now it started to feel to him that this was actually real, and not some fantasy from Colin's dream. He shuddered a little, looked at the girls, and gave them a big false beam of a smile.

'What's wrong with him?' said Rach.

'He's just being, him,' said BB rolling her eyes, but Steph thought differently. She smiled directly at Colin as she looked into his eyes and then repeated his words.

'Come on you lot, this is an adventure for all of us, right? The fun starts here!'

Colin returned her smile.

'Yes, come on you lot,' he said. 'Where's your sense of adventure?'

'Exactly,' said Derek who had overheard part of their conversation. 'Let's continue then.' He was secretly hoping that they were still going in the right direction, and that they would indeed get to their destination before nightfall.

Fortunately, the sun was still relatively high in the sky, a sky that was a perfect blue. Would it be plain sailing? They could see for miles as they climbed further and further into the Bavarian Alps towards Margaret's house and the undoubted warm welcome that would await them there, this would be easy.

'Look,' said BB as the path wended its way upwards. 'This turn goes off to some village, can you see across there through the trees?' she pointed.

'Thank you Briony,' said Deirdre. 'Is it on the map?' she asked Derek.

'Not that I can see, no. The path is here though, but it leads into the woods that is all. I can't see a village marked. Maybe because it is too small, there must be four houses maximum and what looks like a tavern maybe, and that's it. Now shall we go?' he said walking off in the direction that the map was denoting.

They continued along the path. The further they went along it the rockier it became, and more rutted. BB told the gang that she thought it didn't look like it was used very much at all. As a result of the increasing complexity of the terrain, their progress slowed.

Chapter 32

The bus driver had done his job. He did not care to think about what he was sending the innocent party towards. That was not, and could not, be his concern. He would not dwell on their fate, for he was much more concerned about his own. Even so, his heart was a little heavy none the less as he drove away. He had called Margaret from a landline at the café on the banks of Lake Eibsee to confirm that the drop off had been successful. She had seemed pleased, and that was good. He didn't want any fuss or bother coming from her or his master. He just wanted to get out of there, go home and live his little lie of a life until he was needed again.

Margaret had put down the phone on him. She felt the thrill of nearness. Somewhere almost lost inside her, a little voice cried out its protests at what she was doing, but it was, as always, to no avail. She could not go back, she could not fail her master, he had made that all too plain. There was a distinct desperation about this refreshing that was different to any that had gone before in her experience, and she realised that this was what was giving her that additional kick. This was more risky! She used to be so careful, but now she was almost brazen. She was forgetting for a brief moment the dead fish eyed look of her master as she whooped and clapped her hands together.

'I may live, I may die,' she thought. Few could ever feel how she felt at that precise moment intime. Every particle in her body was alive and vibrating. She felt like she was invincible. She danced and pranced until she caught a glimpse of her shrivelled self in the mirror, and then realised like a punch in the stomach that she was just an old woman, an old woman living a lie. She was doomed, she was damned and ultimately trapped. The dichotomy of this scenario was not entirely lost on her, and so she laughed, and she laughed, as if she were mad. She laughed until the tears came and then she sat down with her head in her hands.

After a while she realised that they would all be here in two, maybe three hours. She had to get herself together, make the final preparations. She had it in her mind that the seven were to be in the two largest adjoining rooms, boys in one, girls in the other. The Telling was to be readily placed where it could be easily found. They would then all gather together, as children do when they have a secret. They would read it, and it would be done. The wheels would turn, sleep would come to them, and then the beast, her master, would take their souls by extracting all the moisture from their bodies as they slept. When he was done with them they would be dried up like husks. After that, the merest touch and they would simply turn to dust and disappear with the wind. Her master's power would be restored, and her life would renew once more.

It was inevitable that the police would come to the house afterwards, but no trace would ever be found of the seven. Eventually they would assume (after an exhaustive search of the area), that they had all gone off in the night on some prank into the woods, where they had met some fate that could never be known. A slip, a rock fall perhaps, or possibly an attack by some fiend or wild animal. No bodies would be found, no evidence would be forthcoming, and over time all would be still again.

Margaret would then move to another location somewhere new for the next refreshing. She would leave this house which she would say to the authorities 'Had so many bad memories, those poor children'.

It would then fall into ruin and decay, eventually to be forgotten entirely. This was the way it always was.

The Hutenghast, although weak could still see all here. The seven were close now, the woman Margaret would do what was required, he had made sure of that. He waited impatiently.

In a few short hours night would fall, children would sleep, and he would come for them. How sweet that feeling was, he never tired of it.

Chapter 33

Mr Hart's condition was almost completely unchanged, although the nursing team at the hospital had noticed certain changes to his brain activity, his heart rate and other subtle signs. They were all elevated, and that revealed much. They could perceive a lot from his heightened brain function. It gave them a strong indication that he was struggling with his thought processes. They were sure now that he was totally aware of his situation. They were confident too that he would make a full recovery at some point, but they were still perplexed. There was no reason for him to still be unconscious. His vital signs indicated that he should have awoken way before now, but it was as if he was being held under against his will. There were high anxiety levels present here, and this left them at a loss as to the exact reason why this was happening to him. It was completely unprecedented behaviour; it was as if he were under some influence that was beyond their knowledge.

Mr Hart could never actually see the presence lurking in the shadows, but it spoke to him, not vocally, it didn't have a voice that he could hear exactly, but he sort of felt the words. They came to him without thought, in fact it was like he was talking to himself, but of course he knew that was not the case. The presence was menacing, crafty, and it was dark. Sometimes he had visions, like watching a black and white television. He could see things, a journey, a group of children, some he recognised but could not recall their names, apart from his own son Colin of course. He was anxious for Colin, he tried so desperately to talk to him, but it was simply impossible. All he could do was watch and listen helplessly as the words and visions came to him. They were so vivid that he knew for certain that they were real, the children were travelling to somewhere, and he not only got the impression that this presence was guiding them, but he also knew that when they got to their journey's end it would be waiting there, and that was not good, that was not good at all.

Also, there was an old lady in the picture frame here, she was connected in some way. At first he assumed she was their teacher or perhaps a guide of some kind, but as the time passed by his view changed about her. She was definitely part of the concern here, she was linked to this presence, this creature, in some way. It seemed to Mr Hart that they were almost one being, and not two. She was completely interwoven with this presence. More time passed, and the reality began to dawn on him that she was there as an acceptable face, someone for the children to trust, someone who was to guide them down the wrong path. He thought hard, he was trying to warn his son in some way. Consumed by the effort, all he could hope for was that in some telepathic way, a little of this information would slip through to his son. He could never be sure of this of course, and so night and day he continued on this quest to warn his son Colin. He could feel his own body getting thinner, weaker with the effort, but his mind remained strong. Somehow he had to overcome this hold that was on him. He needed to return to his wife, and to his son, and he needed to do it quickly before something bad happened.

Chapter 34

The Great Being was watching intently. He could see the woman called Margaret. He saw her despair, and also her resolve, he saw her determination as she busied herself getting ready for the visitors to arrive. There was pity for her, but she was lost, there would be no good departure for her, and that was sad, but she was beyond his help.

He watched as she removed the parchment with the black ribbon from its hiding place in readiness to be put in plain sight of the seven children. He could see that she had prepared their rooms, and that they were adjoined. She had thought that when they spied the parchment they would read it together, and then the inevitable would happen. They would laugh and then sleep. The Hutenghast would come for their death and his own renewal.

The Great Being had seen this all play out so many times before. He had wanted to intervene every time, but that was not the way of things. Now he could see the children as they were walking towards Margaret's house, it would not be long now. He knew the Hutenghast was watching Margaret, he was waiting and hoping all things would go well. The Hutenghast was weaker than he had ever been since the dawn of time, he was a desperate thing now, and that pleased the Great Being. He could perhaps finally see an end to all this darkness that had been across the face of the universe.

He could see the boy Colin's father in his unconscious state, scrabbling in earnest like a man trying to climb out of a pit where the walls were perfectly smooth, and impossibly high. It was a seemingly hopeless task for him, but he saw that the man never gave up the struggle.

Love is a wonderful thing he thought. It must be protected, nurtured at all costs. It must never be cast asunder by this abomination ever again.

The Great Being opened his arms wide as he looked down at the scene below. The wind swirled around him, and he picked it up. He moved his arms backwards and forwards like a swaying tree. The winds grew stronger and stronger until all the clouds in the world below moved to the sway of his body. Moisture came from his mighty breath as he summoned them all to him, and the clouds continued to billow and thicken into a dense dark fog.

When he had brought everything under his control, the fog danced and moved downwards, downwards. The travellers far below were still walking bathed in the late afternoon sun…and then the darkness came.

The fog encompassed the group like a blanket. It fell about them, and they were thrown into a darkness like no day that they had ever seen before.

The Great Being did not intervene further, he merely watched things unfold. Control of the heavens was always within his reach; he could use it as he saw fit. He was content and hopeful that this fog would serve its purpose now. It may, or it may not, that was how it had to be. The fate of those below rested on one alone, and it was not to be him. The Great Being did not know who the one would be that would come forward, or indeed how they would complete this impossible task, but everything within him knew that it could be done, it would be done, it must be done.

Chapter 35

The sky was still blue, the sun was warm. V looked up and was surprised to see the clouds darkening behind the mountain that they were walking towards.

'Look at that!' she said, and pointed towards the cloud formation. It was billowing like smoke, it looked like it could be a fire, but it was coming down from the sky not up from the ground.

Everyone looked across to where V was pointing, and they all now saw what she was pointing at as it came their way. A great swathe wrapped itself around the mountain and continued towards them at great speed.

'It's a forest fire!' someone said but before the words had even been completed, they were overwhelmed by it.

Derek had thought that due to the speed of it that there would be a great wind behind it which could be a danger to them. He had shouted 'Down everyone, NOW!' but it was far too late to move. He closed his eyes expecting the worst as the dark engulfed them all. But to his astonishment there was no wind, there was no sound, it was perfectly still, it was just dark, very dark.

All the children were scared, they shouted and screamed, even the Duke twins were scared, but of course nobody could see that. Everyone stayed perfectly stationary, nobody moved a muscle, nobody ran. Why would they? Falling over the edge was a real possibility in the dark.

Deirdre realised at once that she had to calm the situation down, and quickly. They could not afford to panic. She put to the back of her mind how annoyed she still was with Derek and the headmaster as well. Then she addressed the children. 'OK, it's perfectly alright, nothing to be scared of. It's just summer fog. They get it here in the mountains from time to time,' she lied. 'I expect it will pass over soon, best stay perfectly still until it does pass. Everyone take your backpacks off, put them on the ground and sit on them. That way there is no risk of people bumping into each other while it is so hard to see.'

'I've never heard of summer fog,' BB added rather unhelpfully.

'Nor have I,' said Derek. Deirdre could have brained him right there and then.

'Well, it's a fact so just accept it,' Deirdre spat. 'Anyway, whatever the cause, we need to wait for it to pass.'

Colin (who had been walking with Baz and Rich), grabbed their arms and pulled them close. 'This is it guys, it's starting.'

'What's starting?' said Rach who was close by.

'Nothing,' said Baz. 'We were just ..er..arguing,' he added weakly.

'Scared are you Goldilocks?' Keith Henderson was heard to say as the Dukes sniggered in the background, (Goldilocks was his pet name for Barry Gold and of course he didn't care for it much). Baz was just about to open his mouth to retort when Rach said, 'Not necessary Keith, thank you.'

Although she could not see him, or him her. The connection was made. After a few seconds Keith said 'Sorry..Barry.' He cursed himself for reverting to Mr Hyde.

'Better,' said Rach. 'Better.'

The group sat there for what felt like ages and ages, but in reality was probably a mere twenty minutes or so. It was still dark, unchanged.

Their eyes were now more accustomed to the lack of light, and they could make each other out a little, as long as they were within about three or four feet of each other that is. It was eerily quiet, there was no bird song, no animals moved, no trees rustled, it was perfectly calm and still, eerily calm and still.

Deirdre shivered, even though the temperature had not dropped at all, in fact it was still pleasantly warm, but she was aware that, even though they could not see it, the sun was indeed going down rapidly now, and they had to get to their destination and get there soon.

'OK, taking a little longer than I thought to clear,' she said. 'I think we need to start moving. We shouldn't stay here too long. Everyone got your torches?' she said, knowing that this had been on the list of essentials that the school had told them to bring.

'Yes Miss.'

'OK, so backpacks on everyone and let's move on slowly, torches to the front, no waving them around this isn't a game.'

'I think we should go back to the village,' Derek said out of the blue. He had been quiet for some time, practically mute since the fog came.

'No, we are not going back, we got this far, it can't be much further now, the path was a bit rutted back there I know, but it has been OK now for ages and the house must be close by. We have this map to guide us don't we?' she said grabbing it from Derek's hand. 'So, let's use it, that is what it's for after all, isn't it? Just follow the red line, easy peasy.'

Derek could tell she was stressed and annoyed, and he also knew it was directed squarely at him. He mulled it over briefly, he felt that this was the wrong move here to go on, and so bravely, or stupidly (he wasn't sure which) he decided to put his foot down.

'We are going back down to the village. We know the path, we have been on it already and it's maybe a mile down the track, maximum,' he said. 'To be honest we don't know exactly how far there is to go ahead of us, so it is the sensible option.'

'Is it? sensible? Is it?' Deirdre squawked, then checked herself.

'I have the map and I am taking the girls up to the house. If this map is accurate, as all maps are aren't they?' she continued. 'Then it looks like it is less than a mile to go.'

The children shuffled, they were nervous, and they could feel the tension in the air.

'Now Deirdre, er Miss Rhymer, I think we need to stay together,' Derek continued, 'Hand me the map and we will go down to the village, wait for this thing to clear and then continue.'

'It will be dark by then,' said Deirdre 'We don't even know if that is a pub or even if the place is inhabited at all.'

'It could be a ghost town,' one of the Duke twins said, rather unhelpfully. He was universally ignored.

The friction brought on by the responsibility, the stress of the trip to date, and personal feelings tumbled out and carried the conversation forward between Derek and Deirdre to the inevitable point, separation.

They could not agree on the best course of action, and so Deirdre was taking the girls on with the map, and Derek was taking the boys back to the village. Some of the children interjected and argued at this decision, but it was to no avail.

Colin, Baz and Rich huddled close to the girls. But it was Steph who spoke first. 'Colin Hart, I know something is going on, and you three are all in it together. You haven't told me what it is exactly, and that's fine, that is your prerogative. I'm not your girlfriend or anything so you don't have to tell me everything that goes on. But if this affects us as well, and there is actually something to say, then you had better spill it, right now!' she said all in a rush.

The other girls all chimed in, 'Hey what's this all about?' they said.

'Look,' said Colin. 'We can't go against the teachers' can we? So, there isn't time to say much now. I will tell you all about it properly later OK. It's just, well, I've been having dreams. My dad, he comes to me warning me about something, and well this whole trip has been kind of surreal so far hasn't it. Maybe it's connected, maybe not. I don't know but just be careful, and look out for the other girls and for Miss too, she's pretty upset.'

There was nothing more that could be said in that short space of time as they all picked up their belongings to move off.

They had a group hug in the darkness which was now vaguely lit a little by the torchlights.

'Don't worry,' said Steph, 'We'll be OK.'

Colin looked at Steph. Baz at V, BB at Rich. Rachel's eyes scanned around. She saw Keith about ten feet away, and he was looking directly at her. She smiled weakly at him, and he did the same in return.

And so it was that they parted ways. The girls pressed on towards Margaret's house with Deirdre, and the boys went back down to the village with Derek.

Neither Margaret nor the Hutenghast were aware of any problem here. In his wisdom the Great Being had made the fog so that only humans could see it. The Hutenghast was blind to it. As for Margaret, she was no longer a pure human because her soul had already been accounted for, so she could not see it either. She therefore continued with all her preparations for their arrival completely unaware that the visitors had now parted ways. Of the seven chosen ones only four continued on their journey, the other three were moving away from her. The seven souls required for any refreshing had to be male and also female, and so, even though eleven people still travelled towards her, they were all female and as a result, the plans would now inevitably go awry.

What would she when she realised the worst? What would the Hutenghast do? What could he do? 'He could show himself,' thought the Great Being. He could show himself and become vulnerable. He was absorbed with arrogance, which was his greatest weakness, and that would be his downfall too. Everything was going as he had hoped that it would, and he was content.

Chapter 36

As they walked, the four girls chatted about the short conversation that they had just had with the boys.

'What is all this about Colin's dad anyway?' said V. So, Steph told them all about his dad being in hospital in a coma and everything.

'Blimey, poor Colin, I never knew a thing,' said Rach.

'No, and that is how he wanted it, no fuss. He just wants things to be normal. You all know what he is like, not showy or dramatic.'

'Yes that is how he is,' said BB. 'Poor Colin.'

'Well, whatever this thing is, we have to stick together, OK?' said Steph.

'Absolutely!' they all agreed. And so it was that the seven were now vigilant, they were watching, and they would be ready. But as they had now gone their separate ways in the dark, nothing seemed certain anymore.

About half a mile down the track the boys were having a conversation of their own.

'Steph is no mug is she Col,' Rich said. 'She doesn't miss a trick that one.'

'She has been watching us,' said Baz.

'You saw that too?' said Colin.

'Why didn't you tell her what you told me back there?' said Rich.

'Dunno, time didn't feel right I suppose. Wish I had said something now,' said Colin in a quiet voice.

'Well, they know now. Don't worry though, Steph's got BB, Rach and V with her,' said Rich. 'BB makes a perfect wingman, I mean woman,' said Rich. 'She is..'

'Impressive?' said Baz.

'Yes, that's it, she is impressive,' Rich agreed with a broad grin on his face that nobody else could see as he looked away.

They carried on walking, but after a while the dark affected their relatively good humour, and the positivity began to fade as negative thoughts came to the fore. Colin looked across at Mr Ford.

Derek was mumbling to himself as the boys and he all walked back down the track. The fog was still very thick, and their progress was a little slow, but the torches helped light the way. The boys were all pretty quiet now, they were concerned about the situation with the girls going on ahead alone (apart from the Duke twins that is, who didn't care about anything, other than themselves). Derek was also concerned of course, but as we all know, the adult brain can be very stupid and stubborn at times, and both Derek and Deirdre were allowing their own feelings and personal emotions here to cloud their better judgement. The stupidness of it was that they both knew it, and yet still they carried on with their folly just the same.

The Great Being had anticipated all of this. He was therefore not angry with them. It was just the way that all humans were.

'Please Sir?' said Baz, finally plucking up the courage to speak. 'Should we not all be sticking together right now? I don't like us going back and leaving the girls like that, it doesn't feel right.'

Deep in thought, Derek did not hear and therefore did not answer. He continued to mutter to himself, lost in his own thoughts. A touch on his hand shook him from his private malaise, and he looked around to see Barry Gold.

'Yes Barry?' he said.

'Please Mr Ford, can we go back? Back to the girls. This fog may last all night, they might get lost, they might..'

'Miss Rhymer has the map Barry. She has decided to continue on a path that was completely unknown to us. With a map, and in daylight, that is fine of course, but in the dark? Anyway, I was unable to persuade her to come with us, and as technically the girls are in her charge I could not overrule her. So that is how it is.'

He was completely unconvinced as he spoke these words. In fact, he felt all cold and hollow inside. He knew perfectly well that they should never have split up, and that they should all immediately turn around and go after the girls. But something inside was pulling him away, in the opposite direction. He did not know why this was so. He was as worried about the girls and

Deirdre as anyone of course, but it was as if he could not turn back right now even if he had wanted to, (which of course he did). He felt like he was a piece of metal that was being drawn towards a strong magnet, and the magnet was the village. They had to go to the village.

After a moment he said, 'Sorry Barry, the girls will be absolutely fine. Miss Rhymer used to be a troop leader in the Girl Guides and so she is well equipped and more than used to orienteering and such. They will all be fine. As soon as this wretched fog clears we will go back and catch up with them. I expect that they are probably already having something to eat and drink at the accommodation right now as we speak. So come on boys, let's get to that village. Maybe they have a landline there, and we can call the house to make sure that everyone is OK. OK?'

Still lees than convinced, Baz nodded and went back over to Colin and Rich.

'He's determined to carry on, so what can we do?'

'Don't hit me Baz, and this is going to sound really weird,' said Colin. 'Especially as I was the one who was so worried about things going wrong on this trip and all that, but something is telling me that this is what we are supposed to be doing right now, walking away. I know it doesn't make any sense at all, but the thought of turning around and going after the girls right at this moment, in the fog just seems..wrong.'

Rich looked at them both, 'I can't believe I am saying this boys,' he said. 'But I feel it too mate.' He looked at Baz. 'The girls are fine I can feel it. They need to be on their own right now, I can't explain it, sounds mental right? First thing after the fog lifts though, we go, no question, we go. Regardless of whether he thinks it's right or not. Right?' he said inclining his head towards Derek.

'OK,' said Baz. 'I don't like it, but OK.'

Colin nodded in agreement. 'This is so surreal, I feel like we are being guided here. Not in a bad way, something or someone is looking out for us right now. Maybe it's my dad. I don't know, but on this occasion we go on as we are. It's the right thing to do.'

A few feet away Keith Henderson was eavesdropping, as usual. He wanted to say something to the boys but decided against it. He was distancing himself from the Duke twins now, and gravitating more towards the gang. 'If anything happens to Rachel,' he thought to himself. 'Then Mr Ford is going to be in big, big trouble.' He would make sure of that if it was the last thing that he ever did.

The boys got to the turn in the path that they had seen on the way up, and veered off in the direction of the village.

'I hope it is inhabited,' thought Derek. 'Oh, please let it be inhabited.'

They walked on, and slowly the small cluster of buildings that they had spied earlier that afternoon came into soft focus. As they got nearer, Keith Henderson shouted 'Hey, look there is smoke coming from the chimney of the pub!' They all squinted their eyes to focus, and Colin said 'So there is. Come on!'

They all ran the last ten yards. Derek grabbed the handle and flung the door wide open, and they all rushed in.

Chapter 37

Deirdre, much like Derek, was deep in thoughts of her own. 'What am I doing? This is stupid.' She had thought about turning back almost immediately, but she was angry, and also she was determined to show Derek that he was wrong in all this, and that she was right. She walked on with the weight of her foolishness and guilt bearing down on her with a tear in her eye.

As she was thinking all this, the girls were discussing the whole splitting up situation. They were pretty sure that the boys would be OK, they were far more concerned about their own journey into the unknown, and in the dark too. It was therefore decided unanimously, after a short discussion, that one of them would talk to Miss Rhymer about the whole thing. Veronica was chosen for the task, and she sidled over to speak to her. V was just about to open her mouth to say what she had worked out that she wanted to say, and then she stopped short, she turned around and walked straight back over to the others.

'Well?' said Rach.

'I didn't ask her,' she replied.

'Why ever not?' Rach responded.

'Because she is crying, that's why not, OK?' she whispered through clenched teeth.

The girls looked at each other and it was BB spoke first.

'OK, the boys are fine, we know that don't we? Therefore, we don't have to worry about them, do we? Right now, what we need to do is support Miss, and make sure that nothing happens to anyone, and that we get to this house as quickly and safely as we can, OK?'

'Agreed,' they all replied.

'Right, leave this to me,' said Steph walking over to Deirdre as if she was on a mission.

'Please Miss?' she said 'I think the fog is easing a little now. Can I have a look at the map? There was a marker by the side of the path just now,' she lied. 'Maybe it is on the map, perhaps it could show us how far we still have to go.'

Deirdre looked at Steph. 'OK Stephanie,' she said handing it over to her without argument.

Steph pretended to look closely at the map, but she knew that as there was no marker, and that it would not be on the map. She just wanted to break the dour train of thought here, and add a positive spin to the proceedings. That is what her mum always did when her dad was in one of his moods. For example, if he'd misplaced something important, and couldn't find it, or had just played a particularly bad round of golf or something. 'Divert and move on.' That's what her mum called it. And so, Steph had decided to do exactly the same.

'Sorry, no marker on the map Miss,' she said. 'But we've just gone round this bend here I think,' she said pointing to a spot where the red line changed direction a little on the map. 'The house is just ahead of that point, I know it is, take a look,' she handed the map back to Deirdre.

'Yes, I think you are right Stephanie, well done. Come on girls let's get there quickly. Maybe they have a phone, and we can call the village to make sure the boys and Mr Ford arrived safe and sound. I expect they are there already, maybe they are trying to call us right now. Anyway, let's get going. Thank you Stephanie,' she said with a knowing look in her eye.

'She's a bright girl that one,' she thought as they walked on.

Steph had been correct in her map reading (even if it was by chance) because as they rounded the corner the path widened a little and V immediately shouted 'What is that?' in alarm.

'Why it's a statue!' said Deirdre, looking at the stone nymph holding a bowl of fruit or something similar. 'We must be close now.'

Margaret had been at the window, watching and waiting, for several hours. The sun had been getting very low in the sky and although the day was still clear (to her anyway), she was still totally unaware that for the girls and Deirdre it was very foggy and very dark, and that they were diminished in number.

Margaret heard a noise. She looked in the direction that it came from, and a woman appeared. 'That must be the teacher Deirdre Rhymer.' Margaret thought. She was followed by ten girls. Margaret knew which were the four chosen ones, for it was as if a light emanated from their chests, their souls shone out. So young, innocent, perfect. They were finally here!

Margaret expected the male teacher Derek Ford and the boys to come round the corner and into view at any moment. But they did not come! She began to be concerned, and that concern quickly turned to utter panic, as each step that the party took as they neared her house, the skies darkened and darkened, not with night, but with a dense fog. It became denser and denser until it was almost total darkness. She had not noticed at first that the girls were holding torches, but as they neared the house, and the fog thickened, their light became more and more evident. By the time Deirdre knocked at the door, everything was engulfed in this all-consuming fog. Margaret was spooked like never before. This was not the work of the Hutenghast, she knew that. It was Him. The name she did not know, and even if she did, she would not dare to think it, or say it.

All at once, she realised that this was all connected, her master's weakened form, the fisheyes, the uncertainty, and now this. What she was witnessing here was the commencement of battle. Her master and Him. Margaret's very existence now felt like a feather in the wind, and she was plunged into a state of abject fear and panic.

The door knocked for a second time, and summoning all her wits, Margaret went into the entrance hall, and over to the front door. She paused for a moment, took a deep breath, and opened the door.

'Welcome, welcome, my name is Margaret,' she croaked, trying to look normal and sound unfazed. 'Come in.'

They all marched in quietly, and Deirdre turned to the old woman.

'I'm sorry we are a little late, but the weather turned quickly when we were halfway up the mountain track.'

'Summer fog,' one of the girls said.

Thinking on her feet Margaret replied, 'Yes, er summer fog indeed. Glad you made it safely my dears. May I ask where the male children, er I mean the boys are? They are just a little behind you I trust, yes?' she asked hopefully.

'No, they went back down to that village place,' said V.

'That's right,' said Deirdre. 'We will, er, be re-grouping in the morning, as long as the weather clears of course. Do you have a phone that I could use by any chance?'

'Oh no, this can't be' thought Margaret, 'I must make alternate arrangements, and quickly.'

'Not a problem my dear's. I am sorry to say that the phone line is down, the engineer is coming tomorrow to fix it. Now please everyone go through to the library there,' she managed to say, pointing to a door by the stairs. 'Refreshments are waiting, I will go and prepare your rooms.'

She scuttled off at great speed for someone who was evidently very old.

'She's odd,' said BB.

'Don't be rude Briony, she's probably just an eccentric, that's all,' said Deirdre.

'Maybe,' BB replied as they went through into the library, 'But she seemed very on edge about the boys not being here.'

'And the fog,' said Steph. 'The look on her face, did you see it? It dropped like a stone. It was as if she hadn't even seen the fog until we got here.'

Upstairs Margaret was panicking, she had work to do. She wondered if her master was aware of the situation. The thought scared her. Would he think she was failing him? She wanted to run away now, but she was too old, and also she was trapped. There was nowhere she could go, nowhere that she would be safe. Margaret realised that she had no alternative other than to do what she did best, and that was to improvise and survive, survive at all costs.

Chapter 38

Mr Hart was sleeping. He was still unaware of the date, the time of day, or anything else outside of the little capsule that he was suspended in. The only contact with the real world was when he was awake enough to be aware. Aware of the voices and sounds in his room as he lay there all those long months.

As he slept, the being (as he now thought of it), was there, ever present in his dreams. Its malevolence drained him, but the knowledge that this being was intent on inflicting some harm upon his son, was enough to keep his will and energy levels up. He would fight this thing whatever it truly was. It would not defeat him, or be allowed to harm his son. That could not happen.

His body was so weak now, but he was totally unaware of that fact, as he did not use his body anymore. His essence was definitely intact, his brain and his soul were inhabiting a shelter, that was all. Love had kept him sustained, and this being, this beast, this presence that was taunting him, (yes he was aware of that), it was hard to endure, but also, bizarrely, it was helping him too, as it gave him the iron will to prevail.

On this particular day, he was being spoken to (that is the thoughts of words came to his mind as before). The time was close, the presence revelled in the certainty of its tasks nearing completion. Mr Hart realised that this completion, whatever it truly was, was very bad for his son and six others. Seven, seven, seven, this was so strong in his mind. They were seven lambs being led to the slaughter. He was completely helpless, and that absorbed him, not totally though, he still had to fight. The being was weaker though, he could tell that. There was caution now, he was getting scant information, enough to tease and torment, but never enough for him to get a full picture.

The children were close to the place where they were being led to. The intensity of this made Mr Hart's weak body convulse and go rigid as he lay there, he sweated, and noises came from his mouth, but they made no sense to the staff that nursed him. He was just having another bad dream that was all. Poor man!

The black and white image in his mind showed Mr Hart a snapshot of the journey up the mountain that these twenty-two people (including his son), were on. He wondered where this place was exactly, but everything was still so muddled and therefore he could never guess. All he knew for sure was that time was running out now. The twenty-two walked on, the sky was clear, no clouds, sometimes it felt as if he was actually with them, a twenty third person travelling unseen, invisible. He could almost feel the sun on his face as they climbed, and this was a mountain, not a hill.

The being wasn't there with them, it was like he was watching them through Mr Hart's dream. Could he still see them when the dream was over? He did not know. Was his act of dreaming giving the being access to their progress? Or did he have this anyway? Again, he did not know, but he had to see, he needed to know himself.

The dream and the vision continued. Words came to him, 'soul' 'take' 'life' 'death'. Mr Hart did not like these words, but knowledge was everything.

As he watched them walking on, a strange thing happened, things suddenly started to become darker. Mr Hart was no longer with them now, he was back as an observer of the scene in the black and white image once more, but this image was now fading. He could sense that the being was restless, and so he knew that this darkness was not the being's doing, something else, or someone else was at work here. The image faded and flickered, and the being became more agitated. This was good, thought Mr Hart. Whatever was happening now, it was good. Good because although he was losing sight of his son, so also was this thing, and that could only be to their advantage. The image was very faint now, and it flickered one last time before it was gone.

The being roared! He stamped and whirled around. Mr Hart was not frightened, he was elevated. This was a small victory of some kind. A battle was won, but as the being was still here, the war continued, but he was enraged and worried, which was exhilarating to him. He tried to speak, he wanted to shout, to yell defiance, but nothing came, and then all at once, he could feel that the being had fled. He fled like he was running out of a room.

The tight grip that was on Mr Hart, loosened immediately. The being's focus was elsewhere now. Mr Hart had been dropped like a ball, and that was enough to break the tie.

Mr Hart felt like he had been released from the chains that had bound him for all this time. Light came to him. It was blurred, very blurred. Movement within the light caught his eye. It took several moments to realise what this all meant, but then the penny dropped. The light that was above him was not in his mind at all, his eyes were 'opening', he could 'see.'

There was nobody in the room to witness this phenomenon, and so he tried to speak, but although his mouth moved, nothing came forth apart from soft grunts, as he tried hard to form the words. His mouth had forgotten how to work.

He concentrated hard, and then with all his might he tried again. 'COLIN,' he shouted, 'COLIN'. The effort was so great that he slipped back into his mind, and was under once more, but now it was different, he was unshackled.

The nurse on charge, on hearing his cry, ran into the room and just caught a glimpse of his eyes open and alert, but just as quickly as she had seen them open, they rolled up, and he was out again.

'Doctor!' she called. 'Doctor, it is Mr Hart. He is coming round; he is coming round!'

Chapter 39

The tavern had looked quite a substantial building from the outside, but as they entered, the space they now inhabited seemed to be filled in an instant with their arrival. It was definitely a public house of some kind, and there were several rough made tables and chairs scattered around a small inglenook fireplace, and straight in front of them was the bar, above which stood a row of steins where glasses would have been in an English pub. Behind the bar stood a well set man, he was roughly shaven, and had an impressive stand of dark hair for somebody of his age. Derek estimated that he was in his sixties. He was wiping the bar down with a cloth that looked like it had never been washed or wrung out.

'Good afternoon,' said Derek hoping that the man would have a good understanding of English. He heard a chair leg scrape on the wooden floor and noticed for the first time that there were four men sat at one of the tables. They had been hunched over it in conversation when they came in, and so had been fairly inconspicuous before, but now they were all looking directly at Derek and the boys, not in any aggressive way, just curious.

'Good day Sir, gentlemen,' the bartender replied in surprisingly good English. He looked them all up and down. His expression was neutral, and so Derek could not gauge the man at all, but that was not his main concern at that moment.

'Do you have a telephone or a mobile that I could use by any chance?' he asked.

The men at the table had turned back around, and continued discussing whatever it was that was of more interest to them than eleven strangers in their local, ten of which were boys.

'No signal up here Sir,' said the bartender. 'Main phone line is out. Been out for hours now. I expect the telephone company will come by in the next week or so to fix it,' he continued.

'I see, that's a shame,' said Derek, 'You see we need to call someone and, well they are not far away but we can't reach them in this fog, and it's very important that I speak to her, er them,' he blurted out.

'It's the rest of our party, the girls and Miss Rhymer,' Colin said cutting in. 'They carried on up the track to the place we are supposed to be lodging at while we are here hiking,' Derek continued.

'And what place might that be Sir?' said the bartender. 'There's nothing up there but mountains and woods.'

'Alpspitze, it's called Alpspitze,' said Derek.

Silence fell for a few seconds, and then it was quickly broken by the noise of four chairs legs grinding on the wooden floor as the men turned to face them once more. Their previous important conversation with each other, now all forgotten.

'Ah the big house,' said the bartender. 'Nobody goes up there, we don't go up there. Just an old lady there on her own, nobody else. She doesn't like visitors and we don't pry. There must be a mistake.'

'No, mistake,' said Derek. 'The rest of our party are there already, I just wanted to make sure that they had arrived safely, that was all.'

'It's her doing all this,' a voice said. They all turned their heads towards the table where the four men were sitting. One of them had stood up, and he now spoke to them for a second time. 'The phone line down, this fog, it's all her doing. Nothing good comes from that place.'

'That's enough,' said the bartender, but the man continued anyway.

'No Fritz, these strangers need to be told, we don't want trouble coming here.'

'Trouble, what trouble?' said Derek. He could see that the boys were looking worried now, but they remained quiet (Colin, Barry and Richard were waiting to hear whatever this was that they had to be told about).

'It's not just her up there though is it? I've seen a man about the place too, a couple of times, when I've been in the woods close by,' he continued.

'What man?' said Derek.

The man went on to explain what this person looked like.

'The bus driver!' said Rich. 'He just described the bus driver. This is getting weird.'

'We should go,' said Baz.

'No, no, she made the arrangements remember, probably gave him the map too. I'm sure it's all fine,' Derek continued, not very convincingly.

'But it's not just them is it!' the man continued 'There is that other..'

He was cut off from finishing what he was about to say by the bartenders raised voice.

'Enough Hermann, you drink too much. You see things that aren't there, go home now, and sleep it off.' He looked at the other three men sternly. They all stood up and one of them said 'Come Hermann, Fritz will deal with this.'

Without further ado they all walked out of a door at the back of the bar room, and could be seen heading off into the fog.

'Have you seen this fog before?' Derek asked the bartender.

'We get all weathers up here Sir. Now come sit and I will get you some food and drink. It is too late, and too dark to go anywhere tonight. I am sure the weather will be clear by the morning, and you can all be on your way then.'

He went out the back and could be heard speaking to a woman in German, which they all assumed was the cook, and probably also his wife.

'I'm worried Sir,' said Colin 'I thought it was OK us parting ways for tonight, and that nothing was going to happen yet.'

'Yet, what do you mean by yet?' said Derek.

'Oh, nothing, I just meant it didn't feel wrong, but now it does, that's all. Can we leave and go find the girls now Sir?'

'No, I think we have made enough errors for one day. One old woman isn't going to harm anyone is she, and the map showed that they were closer to Alpspitze than we were to all come back here to the village, so I am sure they are all perfectly settled for the night,' he continued.

'So why did we split up then?' interjected Keith Henderson. 'If it was closer to the house than it was to come back down here, why do it?'

'Good question,' said Baz.

'I didn't want to go on in the fog along a track we were not familiar with, but Miss Rhymer was determined to do so. On reflection we should have all stayed together regardless. I apologise for that boys', I really do, but I'm sure that it is all a worry over nothing., so let us have something to eat and drink, get some sleep and start afresh tomorrow, OK? Subject closed!'

There didn't seem much point in pushing the matter any further, and so they all settled down, ate the food, and drank the home-made lemonade. A little later they were escorted through to a room in the rear behind the kitchen by the bartender's wife. It was mostly empty, but the bartender's wife (who spoke no English) had clearly prepared makeshift bedding for them all on the floor. They thanked her, and she nodded and bowed a few times silently, and then left them to their thoughts.

'First thing in the morning, we go, right?' said Rich.

'Right,' the gang agreed. Keith Henderson thought the same thing, but he said nothing. Eventually they all settled down and slept. Outside the stars shone in the sky. The fog had lifted.

Chapter 40

Margaret could hear the girls chattering away in the library on the floor below as she took the parchment with the black ribbon from the place in the bedroom where she had secreted it just a short while before. It was in the room that was to be Steph, BB, V and Rach's room for the night. They had thought that they were all here for a few days to hike the mountain woods and trails nearby, but the plan had been for them to find the parchment that very first night. They would then have read The Telling with the boys, gathered in their little group of seven. 'How convenient,' Margaret had thought at the time. 'So easy.' They would then fall asleep and well, the rest would take care of itself wouldn't it. Her master would come, she would be refreshed, this would be after the police had gone, so could be no suspicion, (they could not see her youth return). After a little more time had passed by and she had been left in peace once more, the driver would be called, and they would go on to the next chosen place. Margaret did not know where that place was to be, but what she did know was that when she closed the door and left Alpspitze, it would be left fully furnished. She would just drive away. When she opened the door of the next place, all her things, her books, her furniture, they would all be there. Perfectly in their place, just like the house had always been that way. It was a courtesy that begged to be questioned, but she was too clever to do such a thing. The master did not like questions, she was there to listen, and to do as she was bidden to do. This courtesy was one of the things that she was given for her duty, along with her longevity. It was a very small thing for the price of one's soul.

The original plan could not happen now of course, the fog had changed all that. They could not be allowed to read the words tonight any longer. She had to stay calm! Tomorrow the male children would come to find them. Then, and only then, could they proceed as planned. One more night, one more day, that was all she had to endure. Twenty-four hours, that was not so bad, she could do that. Her master would understand, she hoped.

She took the parchment that was wrapped in the black ribbon from the drawer in the side table by the girl's beds, and put it inside her apron pocket. She exited the room, and started to walk along the landing. At the exact same time Deirdre was climbing the stairs to come and find Margaret to ask her where the facilities were located downstairs. It had been a long walk, and they were all in need of a freshen up.

A couple of steps from the top of the flight she stopped. There was Margaret coming out of a door a few feet away. She noticed that Margaret looked left and right in a strange way. Deirdre wasn't sure why she did what she did next, but instead of just making herself known, and asking her question, she ducked so that her head was below the banister rail. She could still see Margaret, but she herself could not been easily seen. Margaret walked across the landing towards another door. Halfway there she stopped, looked around for a second time (Deirdre ducked down again), and then she fumbled in her apron pocket and produced what looked like a rolled-up piece of paper tied in the middle. It was brown in colour and so Deirdre thought it must be old. She continued watching as Margaret stooped down. She was out of Deirdre's eyeline now so she could not see what Margaret was doing exactly. After a few moments she stood up. The old rolled up paper was no longer in her hand. She had hidden it! This seemed odd, and so Deirdre waited a few moments longer until Margaret had moved away from the spot where she had paused, and then she made a noise, and moved forward as if she was only just arriving at the top of the stair.

'Excuse me, er Margaret. Is there a washroom downstairs?'

Margaret almost leapt out of her skin. 'Goodness, you surprised me dear,' she said, holding onto the corner of a console table. She looked keenly at Deirdre, who returned her gaze as coolly and innocently as she could muster. 'Can't raise any suspicions now,' thought Margaret, hoping that Deirdre had seen nothing. She gambled that she had not, and replied. 'Yes of course dear, follow me.' Righting herself, Margaret walked past Deirdre, down the stairs, and showed her the way to the cloakroom. 'Here we are dear,' she said. 'Is everything OK, food and drink to your satisfaction I trust?'

'Yes, yes, thank you,' said Deirdre. 'The girls are quite tired, so I expect an early night will do them good.'

'Excellent idea my dear,' said Margaret. 'I am just finishing off upstairs. The rooms will be ready soon. Please rest and eat. I will come back shortly to show you all to the bedrooms.' With that, she turned and walked back up the stairs.

Deirdre was a little intrigued by what she had just witnessed, but her priority was to the girls, they needed food and rest before meeting up with the others again in the morning, as she did herself. Her anger had abated long ago, and she hoped that Derek was feeling OK, and that he was not angry with her. They had both been a little foolish, and a tad reckless too, she was still kicking herself for that error. She would make up for it over the next few days.

In the library the girls were eating sandwiches and drinking lemonade as Deirdre walked back in.

'Did you find the old lady?' said V.

'Margaret? Yes I did, there is a cloakroom across the entrance hall, I have left the door ajar for you. Go freshen up, and I will see you in a few minutes. Margaret is upstairs preparing our bedrooms,' she said.

'She's weird,' said Rach. 'Dear this, and dear that. Who talks like that anyway?'

'Old people do,' said Deirdre

'Do you say dear Miss?' said V with a smirk.

'That's enough cheek thank you Veronica,' said Deirdre with a smile as the girls filed out of the door to go and freshen up.

Deirdre had a proper look around the library, it was quite impressive. A large amount of expensively bound books adorned the shelves. Too many to read in one lifetime she thought. Strange that one old woman had all this. 'Maybe she had a husband who was a professor or something,' she thought. 'Or maybe she inherited them?' Whatever the reason, it was a spectacular sight to the eyes of a teacher. She picked up a book, and inspected the cover. It was bound in thick leather and gold leaf. On the spine was the title in gold. 'Brave New World by Aldous Huxley.' She opened the cover, and it was signed presumably by the author as it read 'To Dearest M. fond regards A.H.'

The book was a first edition, but also specially bound.

'I wonder who M was?' thought Deirdre. 'It couldn't possibly be Margaret as this book was published in 1932. I suppose she could have met him later in life and he gave it to her as a gift then,' she thought. 'After all, he did live into the 1960's, so it was possible.'

If only she had looked at the book next to Brave New World as she returned it to its place on the shelf. If she had, then she would have seen that it too was a leather bound first edition copy, but this one was Bleak House, and it was also signed by the author. 'To Margaret, my friend, my counsel and my inspiration. Charles Dickens 1860.'

Deirdre walked over to a side table. There was a large decanter on it, it was full of a dark liquid, and there were two crystal glasses next to it on a silver tray. She took the glass stopper off the decanter and sniffed the contents. It was brandy, and it was a good brandy too.

Deirdre heard the girls returning, and so she quickly replaced the decanter's stopper and sat back in the chair looking as innocent as she could for the second time in a matter of minutes.

The girls came back into the room, BB was just about to engage Deirdre in conversation, chiefly about all the questions that were still on all the girl's minds, when she felt a presence beside her. It was Margaret.

'Your rooms are all ready for you my dears. Please would you all follow me?'

Rach mouthed 'Follow me my dears,' to Steph, BB and V, rolling her eyes as she did so, and they all sniggered. Everyone followed Margaret out of the room, and they followed her across the entrance hall and then up the stairs to the first floor.

At the top of the stairs Margaret pointed to three doors to the left. 'Those are for the boys when they all arrive tomorrow morning. They are all ready as I was expecting them to arrive with you all my dears. But no matter, what is one more day amongst friends?'

V mouthed, 'Weirdo,' to her friends who all had to put their hands over their mouths to hide their smiles and muffle their laughter. Margaret seemed completely oblivious.

'This room,' said Margaret as she opened the door next to the one that was to be for Colin, Baz and Rich. 'Is for you four,' she said to the gang. 'And this one is for you three, and this one for you three,' she said to the other girls. She looked at Deirdre as she opened the last door on that floor. It was the door nearest to where Margaret had stooped down earlier Deirdre was thinking. She did not look down of course, for that would have been noted by Margaret, and she did not want to draw any attention to the fact that she had been spying on her earlier. Although she did not look, she could tell that there was a carpet runner there.

'This is your bedroom dear,' said Margaret. 'My own rooms are upstairs on the second floor,' she said pointing up the next flight. 'Should you need anything in the night there is a bell here that links to my room.' She pointed to an ornate looking button set in a brass rose that was on the landing wall next to the flight of stairs. 'I will leave you to settle in. There are facilities in all your rooms, so there is no need for any of you to wander around in the night trying to find a bathroom,' she continued. 'I will say goodnight then, and sleep well. Breakfast will be at 8am in the library.' She paused a moment and then said, 'Well goodnight,' and with that she went up the staircase not waiting for any reply.

Deirdre made sure all the girl's rooms were as Margaret had described, and that they all had ensuites, which they did, along with identical beds, all with identical crisp white sheets.

'Goodnight girls,' she said. 'It has been a very long day. Tomorrow after breakfast, as long as the fog has cleared, which I am sure it will have. We will go down to the village to meet up with the others, OK?'

'Yes Miss,' they all replied as they closed their bedroom doors. It was quite late now, and they were all tired, so it was not long before they were all asleep. The beds were extremely comfortable they all realised, and the pillows were incredibly thick and soft, in fact everything was clearly brand new. Nobody stirred until the morning came knocking at the window. Nobody that is except for Deirdre.

She lay there wide-awake staring at the ornate rose and chandelier on the ceiling, it was ridiculously out of place in such a simple bedroom. Deirdre thought that it belonged in a large dining room, or a ballroom, or somewhere like that. 'A larger room than this anyway,' she thought because it was huge. Fortunately, the ceiling was around ten feet above the bed, and so there was no fear that she could bang her head on it in the night, should she have need to 'wander' as Margaret had put it.

Deirdre heard Margaret moving around in the rooms above, but eventually all was quiet. She thought about Margaret, she was an intriguing woman, for clearly she really was all on her own in this big house, and yet she had prepared all the food, made up multiple beds, too and everything was perfectly done. It was quite amazing that a woman who was in her eighties still had so much energy. 'A nervous energy though,' thought Deirdre. Margaret was definitely more than she appeared on the surface. Deirdre wondered why she would want to still be doing all this sort of thing at her age. What could possibly be her motive? It was a massive house too, a major thing to tend to for anyone alone, and she was at least eighty-five if she was a day she thought. Margaret was weird, she had to agree with the girl's sentiments there, but she was also formidable, even though she looked frail and old. She was, Deirdre thought, as sharp as a tack and obviously very resourceful with it.

As she lay there thinking her mind wandered to the events that had happened earlier that day. How could she have been so stupid as to go off with the girls alone. She should have listened to reason, as should Derek too of course. On reflection it was clear that the most sensible thing was for them all to stick together. She still felt that going back to some village which may be deserted still seemed wrong to her, but she also knew that the decision should have been a joint one between Derek and herself. They should all have either gone back, or all moved on, together. Now they were separated, and although she was here with the girls, she felt very alone as she lay there. She was very restless, so she tried to relax without success. 'I need a drink,' she thought.

The decanter in the library came to mind. 'I will go down, and have one drink of brandy to settle me down, just to help me sleep.'

She got out of bed and crept over to the door. For some reason she half expected it to be locked, but it wasn't of course. She opened it as quietly as she could. Across the landing and down the stairs she went, luckily there were no loose boards to creak, and there was a thick tread on the stair runners, so she moved silently. All that could be heard was the tick of a grandfather clock that was on a halfway mini landing at a point where the stairs changed direction down to the ground floor. It felt like the face of the clock was looking at her as she passed it. She brushed that aside as guilt for what she was about to do. She carried on.

Eventually she got to the library door without alerting Margaret. She stopped to listen. All she could hear was the clock, and then she felt a shiver, it was like there was somebody there, watching. She spun round expecting to see Margaret with an accusing face, but there was nobody there. She let out a long sigh, and that was when she realised that she had been holding her breath practically the whole way down the stairs. It was colder down here, and eerie too in the dark. She still felt sure that someone was watching her, which made her feel uneasy, but she shrugged it off. She needed a drink. Opening the library door, she walked in. Even though she felt uneasy, she still shut the door behind her. She turned on a sidelight nearby which illuminated the room sufficiently for her to navigate her way safely and quietly to the table that had the brandy on it.

Half an hour later Deirdre left the library, carefully turning out the light and closing the door behind her. The only evidence that she had been in there at all was that the decanter was now half empty. The brandy in it had been so smooth, so warming and comforting, that one small glass had not been nearly enough to take the edge off her anxieties. Three full glasses later, she was warm inside and calm. She sat the glass down, wiped it carefully to remove any traces of use, and rather unsteadily walked to the door, then out, and up the staircase once more. Although she was a little wobbly and lightheaded, she still moved without a sound. A dark shape caught her eye, and she jerked her head around but there was nothing. Going past the reproachful grandfather clock for a second time, she stuck her tongue out at it in a defiant way, much as she would have done as a child. At the top of the stair, she turned right again and tiptoed past the girl's bedrooms, they were clearly all fast asleep. 'Lucky them,' she thought.

As she got to her own bedroom door she tripped over the edge of the carpet runner that led up to the second floor, lifting a corner of it as she did so. Bending down to put it right, she noticed that the floorboard underneath it was raised a little and the edges were rough, like it had been removed and replaced many times. She pulled back the carpet enough to see the board, it was quite different to the rest of the floorboards. At first she thought there was a knot in it, but on closer inspection she could see it was a hole that had been drilled into the wood. She put her finger in and pulled, the small board came out easily in her hand, and she looked into the void. There was the paper. She picked it up, it was some type of parchment, and what tied it in a roll was a black ribbon. 'Probably old Margaret's will,' she thought. 'Or a treasure map!'

In her drunken state she was not thinking of the consequences of her actions. She replaced the board. She put the carpet back as it should be. The parchment was in her left hand, and so she opened the bedroom door with her right. Turning on the very dim side light, she climbed back into bed, and carefully undid the black ribbon. There was just enough light to read, she unrolled the parchment. The words on it were written in black ink, and in an old script. It was easy enough to decipher the words. Being a little the worst for drink, she read it aloud, as you tend to do when you are a little tipsy. Unbeknown to her, that was her first real, and fatal mistake.

The Telling

From faded fable and old folklore
From whispered words and thoughts no more
The fear of death from whence he came
The Hutenghast it is his name
He can sense your moisture and see your soul
Wherever you are there's no control
He knows too much to let you go.

He's from the mountains and the wood
He's always near whether you're bad or good

And while you sleep he'll find a crack
Creep into your dreams, there's no way back
Whether newly born or bent and old
The Hutenghast will seek your soul
He knows what makes you tick.

You can hide in a fortress, or build an ark
Turn off the lights and in the dark
He'll creep along like a willowy ghost
And suck the moisture from your throat
He'll whisper gently in your ear
There's no escape, and in your fear
The life is drained from you.

Cunning like fox and strength of bear
With slavering snout and matted hair
Extended arms and steel like grip
Scratch and scrape and chip chip
The Hutenghast can smell your soul
Invading your dreams his endless goal
His only focus is your demise
He sees the moisture in your eyes
He'll never let you live.

Both the jaded of heart and the shining brightly
The Hutenghast prowls for you nightly
You may pray or cower in your bed
Either way you'll end up dead
Devoid of moisture and like a prune
Your loved ones find you in your doom
Another lost to him.

Most stories end on a note so bright
Past darkened days into the light
But the tale of the Hutenghast is forlorn

There is no redemption or sunny morn
For no God or Devil knows his birth
He's not of the sky or bound by earth
He's of our dreams and this I say
The Hutenghast may pass your way

And if he does no knight will come
No rescuer, for his will be done
No wringing hands or pious thoughts
Can help you now for all is nought
The Hutenghast has come a calling
No point in screaming or cat-a-walling
He's locked on to your very soul
No heavenly or earthly hole
Of refuge is there for you now.

For the Hutenghast has come your way
Your moisture gone, your flesh decay
Off now you go to endless night
All fear is gone, your lifeless flight
The Hutenghast has passed on through
He came for me and now it's you
Watch out! Here he comes.

He sees you in the dead of night
You can't escape though you think you might
As no heavenly body, or earthly form
Can stop him now, your parents mourn
Tomorrow when they think you'll wake
Mother or father will not mistake
Your shrunken form inside your bed
Now endless screams will fill their heads
The Hutenghast has passed your way
Your wasted life's all gone, decay.

But there is a way to avoid this fate
This written word it is the bait
For The Hutenghast to be called to arms
And if he's not, there can be no harm
Only these words spoken bring the dread
Please read them only in your head
For if these words be voiced aloud
All who hear them will be cowed.

The Hutenghast he will not rest
Till the moisture's gone from every breast
Of all who hear and all who know
He'll seek you high or look below
No hiding place whether earth or sky
Will shield you now as by and by
The hunt is on for you!

Stay awake!, or his will be done
As eyelids shut, and dreams they come
The Hutenghast will be on his way
To drain the life from all who lay
Upon their beds in fitful sleep
Into your dreams he will creep
Your moisture is his greatest prize.

These written words they hold the key
Destroy them not, or all will see
That the Hutenghast cannot be sated
Neither all your love nor all your hatred
Can hinder now or stop the end
Of all that you call foe or friend.

So, bury it quickly, or find a nook
Hide it where no one can look
And as your moisture drains away

And your wasted life falls to decay
One solitary crumb of comfort find
The knowledge that no one left behind
Beyond whom heard these words gone past
Need fear the tale of The Hutenghast!

'What is this?' she thought. Her mind was dulled by the alcohol, and she hadn't really taken in what she had actually just read. It was a poem of sorts she realised that, but it was just mumbo jumbo. 'Margaret really is weird,' she thought, she let the parchment drop to the floor, it coiled back up into a roll as it did so. 'The Hutenghast, what is that?' she thought. 'It sounds like a ski slope.' She laughed to herself, and then her eyelids became heavy, her head began to swoon as the alcohol took effect. As she was dropping off to sleep, she realised that the parchment needed to be put back into the cubby hole again, but she was too far gone to awaken again now. Her eyelids flickered one last time, and then they closed. Within seconds she was asleep, and she was damned.

Outside the sky was full of stars and the fog was no more. The Great Being looked down, he saw Deirdre and knew what was to be her fate. He could not prevent it.

Chapter 41

The Hutenghast had abruptly left Mr Hart's dream earlier. He had then prowled around in the void waiting for Margaret to sleep. He could not waste energy appearing to her in body, and so he waited in anger until she slept. She told him of the fog, also the separation of the male and female chosen ones too. He had himself been unaware of the fog, and also of the separation. It vexed him greatly. He realised that The Great Being was behind all this, and he was afraid of that fact.

Margaret had a plan. 'Just one more day,' she had said. 'Patience master,' she had pleaded. He wanted to strike her down to dust, but that would have achieved nothing, and it could also bring about his own end. Reluctantly, he had listened. He reasoned with her logic, and he accepted Margaret's plan. The Great Being may be looking now, but he could do no more than watch, and play with his clouds. 'I will prevail here, you can't do anything,' he raged in his thoughts. Margaret could not hear his thought, but he knew that 'He' could. 'Damn you!' he thought.

Then he felt the words. Someone was speaking them. A rush of excitement came. 'The words are being spoken,' he told Margaret in her slumber. 'No master. That cannot be, for they are now hidden.'

'The words are being spoken!' he repeated, and then he was gone. Margaret could not waken herself because it was not time for her to do so. She slept on until morning. Meanwhile the Hutenghast moved.

Deirdre had been asleep for a while, slowly the thoughts and visions of dreams came to her. At first they were as normal as any dream, just thoughts of the day, childhood memories, Derek, the children, many things flitted through her mind like a kaleidoscope.

Then the beast came crashing in as if he had ripped the curtains down in her head. He moved towards her, tall and gangling, his long arms and legs moving with intent, they were hairy. His extended fingers twitched, and his mouth was open showing human white teeth within snout of mouth. His lips were full and bulbous. His nostrils flared.

Rigid with fear, Deirdre could do nothing but look into this creature's eyes which were impossibly dark and dead. As he came toward her, the words she had spoken became real. She knew his name, and it froze her whole being. He had come for her! And she was as helpless as a new-born baby. Without uttering a word, he clasped her head on either side with both his hands, his thumbs were across her forehead, and his warm fingers wrapped around her head. They met at the back, forming into a powerful lock. He did not crush her, as she had thought that he might do in her madness. No, he merely pulled her toward him, much as a lover would do for a tender kiss. But this was no tender kiss. His head came close, she could feel his breath, it was colder than ice. He clamped his lips over her mouth tightly, and his cold breath entered Deirdre. He drew it out again, deeply. Much as a needle enters the bloodstream, and then sucks out the blood. This cold rush gushed into her lungs, and then began to withdraw. It was not like being winded though, this was as if everything was being withdrawn. Her entire essence was now leaving her.

Thoughts too terrible to write here went through her mind as she was drained away. She was asleep but she knew that this no nightmare, it was real. That was the last sane thing that went through her mind, the horror of what befell her took the rest away! By the time her eyes were shrunken, and her body had shrivelled. Her soul had exited her wasted form, she was beyond any thoughts. She was fully gone, and nothing but the husk of her remained.

The Hutenghast, his work done, left her there. He was stronger now after his nourishment, but this had been no child. It was a woman, and so the life force in her was weaker, It was insufficient. He realised that he still needed to take all of the seven. This was enough merely to aid him in furthering his quest, as some of his former powers had now returned to him. His eyes flickered like flame once more, and he was hungry. He returned to Margaret. He told her of the transfer. She knew what had to be done. As the sun rose once more, she awoke. The sky was clear, and she moved quickly.

Chapter 42

Margaret went downstairs quietly, and entered Deirdre's bedroom. She did not look at her, she never liked to look. Once was enough. The first time, out of curiosity she had looked, but after that she did her best to avert her eyes as much as she could. She didn't revel in the mess and mayhem. She performed her tasks, and she received her reward for it, that was all she wanted. In between refreshing's she chose to not think of it, if at all possible. It was all very ghoulish, and she was a cultured woman, (well she had been once upon a time), and a trace of that woman would always remain while she still lived.

The task was different now, more difficult, she had to think. How could she get these children together, unconcerned, and to then read the Telling? The woman Deirdre was gone, but something still remained of her, and that had to be disposed of. These children would never comply without her, it was impossible. What of the man, Derek? What would he do? What could she do to make it right? The last thing that she wanted was for them to see the remains. They needed to be disposed of, but first she had to take the parchment before the girl children saw it. They may try to destroy it, and that could not happen. She grabbed it up, and tied the black ribbon around it once more. She left the bed untouched, and exited the room to replace the parchment in its hiding place under the board beneath the runner.

As she turned around to go back into the bedroom, she was confronted by the girl Stephanie, who was just about to enter Deirdre's room. Margaret froze, all her guile now gone, there was nothing that she could do now to stop this runaway trainwreck she thought.

'Miss?' said Steph.

Margaret barred the open door.

'Let me in!' said Steph immediately realising something was wrong.

'You can't go in there, she's unwell. I will call a doctor, go back to your room, NOW!' Margaret flustered. She was strong for an old woman, but Steph was young and quick. She dummied

Margaret, and barged past her into Deirdre's bedroom. She could see a shape under the covers. Margaret grabbed her arm, but Steph was not to be drawn away here. She whipped back the covers to reveal the wasted form that lay in the bed. It did not look human at first, although the shape had the arms and legs, and the bodily appearance of one. This all happened in a fraction of a second, she saw what looked like a mummified body, but it had Miss's necklace around its neck and her ring on its wasted finger. She realised that this was...

'BB!!' she screamed at the top of her voice 'HELP ME, V, RACH, HELP!!'

All nine girls rushed out of their bedrooms, past Margaret and into the room.

They saw Deirdre and screamed, and yelled, and cried. Margaret was shell shocked, she quietly and quickly withdrew, locking the door behind her.

'Master, I need you now! Come to me! Help me!' she cried.

With some of his strength now restored The Hutenghast could see what had happened here. He realised that now there was only one option left to him. The Telling could not be used anymore, that was clear. He had to use what can only be used but once. In all the millennia that had passed before, he had never needed to use this. It was the last resort, and he had no other option now, and so he took it.

Appearing in body on the staircase beside Margaret used much of his reserves, he held what can only be used once in his hand, he put it to his side, and it disappeared into his torso. Margaret was in front of him, the children's screams could be heard behind the locked door. He did not speak, he moved towards Margaret, but he did not take her as you may expect that he would, this was no charging of his life force, this was the last throw of the dice.

Margaret closed her eyes as he walked through her. When he came out the other side, his appearance was that of the woman Margaret, but her eyes were now impossibly dark and lit like a flame that danced at the edges. Where Margaret had once stood, there was a dust on the floor. He had taken her early, there was no transition here, his last servant was now gone. She was part of him now, and he held her form. It was needed.

He opened the door which was being pounded by the girls in their hysteria, and he spoke, 'Silence now, all will be well.'

It was not Margaret's voice that they heard come from her mouth, it was another's voice. It was dark, and it was mesmerising. Stunned into silence, they just stood there. The person that looked like Margaret now waved a hand and spoke once more.

'Sleep, not slumber
Lie, not rest
You are here
At my behest
Words of death
Words of life
May not be used now
Come the knife
But not yet children
One to four
You I have
But I need more
When the three
Come here for thee
They will answer
To knife and me.'

He withdrew the hidden knife from inside his body, and he waved it over his head, just once. All the girls slumped to the floor, as if dead (although they were not, yet). Margaret's body picked the chosen four up two at a time, one under each arm as if they weighed no more than straw dolls, and then took them down to the basement of the house. He laid them down on the floor there. The others were left where they fell. 'I will deal with them later,' he thought. He could sense that the male children were on their way to him now, and so Margaret's body waited there, with the four sleeping ones in the basement. It would not be long now.

Chapter 43

The boys looked out of the tavern window as the sun peaked through the trees.

'It's all clear outside, time to move?' said Colin.

'Breakfast first?' said one of the Duke twins.

'No, Colin is right. Get you things together boys we are leaving, right now.' said Derek. It was time to get things under control. This whole trip had been a complete mess, they all knew that. He didn't care if they left Bavaria today. He didn't care if the Headmaster gave him the sack. All he cared about was getting everybody together and leaving this place, all twenty-two of them, today. They would go get the girls and Deirdre, and then they would go straight back down the track to Lake Eibsee without further delay. Once there, he would call Super Mario, and then they would all get the hell out of Bavaria.

Derek paused for a moment as he watched the boys gather their things. Who knew what lay ahead, and going into battle on an empty stomach was not a good idea, and so he relented.

'OK, boys a quick breakfast. We need our strength, and then we go!' he said.

Breakfast itself was a meagre affair, barely worth the bother, but they all ate and drank quickly, 'All very German,' thought Derek.

It consisted principally of pumpernickel and warm milk. The boys ate just enough, as did Derek, they were all very eager to be on their way.

'Thank you for your hospitality,' Derek said to the bartender and his wife as they waved them off at the door. The bartender had tried to persuade them to go back down to the café beside the lake below and call the authorities from there to come and assist before they went to Alpspitze. Derek had questioned him on why he thought this was necessary in his view, but he just clammed up. It was clear to Derek, and also to the boys, that he was not going to be drawn further on what had been said by Fritz the night before, and why he thought that it was not a good idea to simply go up to Alpspitze to meet the girls as they planned.

'He knows, or thinks he knows that something may have happened last night, I can tell,' Colin said to Baz and Rich. 'This is what I have been worrying about all this time. What I can't figure out though, is why it seemed not to be such a bad thing to us yesterday afternoon. You know, us coming here and the girls carrying on, after Sir and Miss fell out. If anything has happened I will..'

'Hold on there tiger,' said Rich. 'I still feel that it's all OK, I am sure all this is just local talk. They are probably all bored out of their minds most of the time. Just made-up rubbish, that is all it is.'

'I hope you are right,' said Baz. 'I for one will be happy when we get there, and get this over with. I think we are all at a point where we just want to get the girls, and go back to civilisation pronto. I don't want to walk round these mountains anymore. I think even sir wants to just leave now too, and who can blame him.'

'He is worried about Miss…they are an item after all,' said Colin.

Seriously? You mean?..' said Rich, tailing off and not wanting to voice the actual words, as Derek was close by.

'Yep,' said Colin, 'You two never notice anything do you.'

'We are not as nosey as you are if that is what you mean,' said Baz.

'OK, time for a reality check,' said Colin. 'Baz, you like V, and she likes you, right?'

Baz looked sheepish but nodded after a few moments.

'And you,' he said looking at Rich. 'BB and you, it's pretty obvious mate.'

Rich flushed.

'OK, well in that case you and Steph are like joined at the hip too, so what's your point,' said Rich. He sounded a little annoyed but the other two knew he was just a little self-conscious about his feelings regarding BB.

'Even Rach, you know she has a thing for..,' Rich jerked his head towards Keith Henderson, who from his expression they could tell, had been listening in to their conversation the whole time.

'My point is, we all care, right?' said Colin, ignoring the fact that Keith was clearly listening. 'Whatever is up there we deal with it, OK?'

'OK,' they replied.

'Come on boys,' said Derek, 'I think we are almost there now.'

He was walking at a very brisk pace and some of the boys were struggling to keep up, but the urgency of it all had crept into everybody by now, and they pushed on up the steep track. Bizarrely nobody had mentioned about how clear the morning sky was today, and that was because nobody really cared, they were just glad that they could see without the need for torches. It made things feel more normal. Yesterday afternoon, after the fog came down, everything had been so surreal. Today's reality seemed so vivid, and yesterday just felt like a bad dream. If it wasn't for the fact that only eleven people were on the walk up to Alpspitze, they could almost have thought that it really was just something they had all dreamt the night before. But it wasn't, and they really had separated yesterday, and that was wrong. Today they would make everything right again.

There was a sharp turn ahead on the track, and as they went around it, they saw the statue.

'We must be close now,' said Derek.

'There,' shouted Keith pointing ahead. They could all make out through the pines a stone building.

'That must be the house,' said Derek. 'OK, I will go first, you boys all wait here.'

'Not a chance,' said Colin. He had never been so forceful. He had never answered back to an adult before, but he was going to get the girls, and nobody was going to stop him.

'We are coming too,' said Baz and Rich together.

'OK,' said Derek. He reasoned that now was not the right moment to argue and waste time, and he knew that. 'The rest of you wait here, try and get a signal on your mobiles, it's clearer up here you may get through. Come on then you three, stay behind me,' said Derek, and they made their way through the trees, and into the clearing in front of the house.

The house itself seemed surprisingly out of place. Architecturally it was early Georgian in style, English or French perhaps, it was certainly not German. It was a relatively large house, and it had an austere look about it. There were no flowers or any ornate topiary anywhere to be seen. Normally there would be gardeners and borders and beauty outside this type of property, but Alpspitze was just 'there' like it had grown out of the ground, as if it were a big weed. Derek felt a chill, his hair stood on end, and he shivered. He didn't like the feeling of this place at all, and for the first time that day he felt truly uneasy, he was worried. He wanted to go on alone, but he had to admit to himself that having the three boys with him was a sort of comfort too. What he did not know though was that Keith and the Duke twins were following them all at a safe distance. Keith had wanted to go after them alone, but the Dukes could sense this was going to be interesting, and they wanted to see whatever was going to go down. Reluctantly he went with them leaving just four boys waiting by the statue.

'This is fun,' said one of the Duke twins, and his brother agreed. Keith wanted to tear a strip off them so badly, but he didn't want them to figure out his real intentions here. He wasn't sure how he felt about all this, he had spent so much time just being insular, and worrying about other people was not something he was used to feeling. He knew that he felt concern for Rachel, she was kind, but the others? He wasn't sure about that. But, as for fun? No this was definitely not fun. The Duke twins didn't care about the girls, or him, or anybody else either, apart from their mother perhaps. She always seemed numb and neutral whenever Keith had met her. He didn't take to her, but then again, he didn't take to anybody, apart from Rachel that is. He was not going to wait with the others by the statue like a lemon, he was going to find out what was going down here.

Would he jump in and show his feelings if that were needed? 'No,' he thought. 'I can't do that, not here, not now.'

Derek and the boys had reached the front door now, and it was ajar. Not seeing the need to knock he pushed it open, and it answered back with a creak. They walked in. 'Anybody here?' he said in a loud enough voice so that it could be heard from anywhere in the house. They all waited for a reply, holding their breath, but not a sound came back. All they could hear was the tick of a clock, nothing more.

'Hello,' shouted Colin, 'Steph.. BB.. Rach.. V? Are you here? Can you hear me?'

From the basement Margaret's body felt a thrill as the boy spoke. It was the tormented one's son. He had so enjoyed their time together, but that was in the past now. Four he had with him, the other three were now here, in the house, he could feel them, almost touch them. He wanted to run up the stairs and grab them, but they were not alone. The man was with them, he had to wait. The man would see the husk of the one he had taken; it was his woman. His reason would go, he would panic, and then run to get the authorities. He would not leave the other female children there alone Margaret's body had reasoned. So, he will let the three stay behind, and then I will take them. This was all so unexpected. He had assumed that they would all come together, maybe even with the men from the village, but they were alone, just four people. 'They are such fools,' he thought. 'Soon they will be mine.' He put his hand to the knife, it was throbbing in his side. For millennia it had been waiting, now finally it was time for it to do what it was intended to do, what it had been made for. This was the last resort, the silver bullet, and the time was close.

Derek and the boys went into all the rooms downstairs one by one. Everything was in its place, there were no signs of any struggle. It simply looked like nobody was at home. The door had been ajar however, and so someone must have come in, or left in a big hurry. The girls may have left, but they would have met them down the track, that was for certain. Clearly they had not done that, and so, they had to still be here, somewhere.

'Let's go upstairs,' said Rich.

They made their way across the entrance hall, and started walking up the stairs. Past the disagreeing clock, and up towards the first-floor landing.

'Look that door is open,' said Baz as he pointed to the room that Deirdre had slept in the night before. Derek was in the lead, so he got to the door first and pushed it wide open.

Chapter 44

Mr Hart awoke for the second time just a short while after he had unknowingly alerted the nurse. He blinked, and he opened his eyes. He saw a face for the first time in six months. It was a woman, and she was crying, but she was not sad, she was happy.

'Hello love,' said Mrs Hart. 'I don't know what to say, I have missed you so much, we have missed you. It has been so long.'

'Colin,' croaked Mr Hart.

'He can't be here I'm afraid, he's on a school trip. We told you about it while you were asleep, but you probably didn't hear us.'

'Colin,' he repeated. 'Danger, Colin, is in danger.' His eyes closed once more, and he was asleep again. Nothing came into his dream this time as the being had left him, and it wasn't ever coming back.

He could not waste more time sleeping, the being no longer had need to torment him now, and that was very troubling. He did not know much, just fragments, but even if they made no sense to anyone, he still had to wake up and tell his wife everything. He concentrated hard, his head swooned, and he felt like he was being sucked back into a whirlpool whilst swimming, trying to get away. This black veil that had been over him these past months had to go. He could not allow himself to drift back there again, not when his son was in danger. Slowly, slowly he moved away, leaving the whirlpool behind him. His arms and legs burned with the effort of it, even though in reality he was barely moving on the bed, it was all in his mind. His will was pitted against this black malaise, the coma that had held him. Enough was enough, with one last great effort, he was free, his eyes opened wide, he focussed them on his wife, who was still standing there looking over him. He opened his mouth and this time the words came out freely, it was a great relief, but the reverie could wait. He had a tale to tell and there was not much time left to tell it.

After what seemed like hours, but was actually only around ten minutes, Mrs Hart was fully informed of everything that Mr Hart had to say, and scant as it was, it made a lot of sense to her. She had seen the weight of concern on her son's shoulders recently, the lack of sleep, she had heard his calls in the night when he had the bad dreams, (but he was not a baby, and she had not wanted to smother him), if he wished to talk, he knew where she was, that was how she had approached it. Now though, she wished that she had said more, but rather than dwell on the what if's, ever the pragmatist, she was immediately on the move. Moments later she was calling the headmaster's office. It was the holidays, and so she was not necessarily expecting anything other than an automated reply. So, it was a great relief when she heard an actual voice on the other end. The added bonus was that it was the actual headmaster himself! He had popped into the office to do some work, and now he was being given a great stream of information from Colin's mother. A lot of it didn't make much sense, but that little voice that we all have at the back of our minds was tapping away at him.

The trip, the change of arrangements, everything being paid for, not going to the planned place. Not only had he not checked this himself, he had actually sanctioned them going to some place that was not even on a map! His blood went cold.

He hung up the phone and called Watts Coaches. Their driver was staying nearby he remembered that, and so he would be the nearest person to them, and also he was the last known individual to have seen them. Maybe he could tell him something.

The next call was to his secretary.

'Daphne,' he said. 'Can you come into the school, straight away if possible. Yes, thank you. We have some urgent phone calls to make.'

Chapter 45

The bedroom door opened a little, and then came to a stop. There appeared to be some obstacle in the way that was preventing them from getting into the room. Derek pushed harder, and the door yielded. Feeling some trepidation, he walked in, the three boys were all practically tripping over his coat tails behind him. That was when they saw the six bodies on the floor.

The initial shock of the scene before them quickly turned to concern as the group realised with great relief that the girls were in fact still alive. Derek bent down and checked their vital signs. They all appeared to be in no distress and were breathing quite normally, it was just as if they were sleeping. But they were not sleeping in the normal sense, for they could not be aroused. No amount of talking, or shaking could wake any of them. They were completely out of it, just as if they were all in a deep trance. Of course, the boys noticed immediately that the four girls they were most concerned about were not here, but before they could carry on looking around the house for them, they had to help Derek move the prostrate bodies. They were laying together in a heap, two of them were actually on top of each other. It looked just as if they had dropped to the floor instantaneously, a quick multiple event of some kind. It was all very concerning for everyone.

'Get some water from the sink please Barry, I will splash it on their faces to see if will help bring them round,' said a clearly shocked Derek. Baz did as he was asked, he went around the bed and into the ensuite where he found a glass next to the sink. He filled it with water and came back into the bedroom. Passing by the bed for a second time, he noticed that the duvet was very crumpled. It looked like somebody may still be underneath it. Very cautiously he pulled it back to see if one of the gang was in there. What he saw made him drop the glass, water cascaded everywhere as it clattered on the wooden floor. Baz let out a loud, terrified, and almost unearthly scream.

'Blimey! You scared me half to death,' said Derek. 'What's wrong with you Barry, did you see something in the ensuite?'

Baz could not speak for a few seconds as the full horror of what he had just seen sank in. He had witnessed something that no child should ever have to see. He was a bright lad, and even in that very short space of time, he had seen enough to know what or rather who that 'thing' under the covers was.

'Spit it out boy, what is it.'

'Err..err,' was all he could say.

Colin quickly assessed the situation; he had seen Baz pull the covers back out of the corner of his eye as he was helping Derek uncouple the last two girls from their tangled heap. He stood up, and went to draw back the duvet.

'NO, DON'T DO THAT!' screamed Baz, his eyes were wild, and he grabbed Colin's arm, and pulled it away with tremendous force, almost flinging him to the floor.

'What the hell is going on here!' said Derek. 'We have a serious situation, and I need you three to help me. Now calmly Barry, please, can you express what has caused you to behave this way?'

'Miss!' was all he could say. 'It's Miss, under the duvet, but she's...gone.'

'Deirdre?' squeaked Derek as he stood and went to pull back the cover.

'NO, PLEASE, don't Sir, she's dead. Her body, it's horrible. She is all dried up like a mummy, but it is her, I know it is. We need to find the other girls now!' He was in a blind panic.

Derek's face crumpled. Even though he hadn't seen her himself, he just knew that Barry was right. With a valiant effort, he gathered all his inner strength and then said to Barry, 'Please, you go with Colin and Richard to look for the other girls. I will tend to things here.'

'Please don't look Sir, you mustn't touch her. Promise me you won't,' he said.

Colin and Richard were very quiet, totally shell shocked. They followed Baz out of the room, and they all quickly and quietly started to search the other rooms on that floor.

Derek was shaking, but he laid the girls together side by side on the large rug next to the bed. He checked their vital signs again calmly, they were still as if asleep, breathing normally, temperatures were fine, pulses were normal. He moved to the bed, took a sobbing intake of breath, and very gently eased back the cover.

He almost collapsed, he stifled a scream, or was it a sob, or a roar. He wasn't sure what would have come out of his mouth if he hadn't stopped himself. He had prepared himself, those few seconds as he saw to the girls, but as he stood there now looking at the shrunken form before him that was once Deirdre, he was completely bereft. Tears came stinging to his eyes, and he balled up his fists so hard that his fingernails cut into his palms, the blood from them dropping onto the bed linen, and the wooden floorboards.

'Oh Deirdre,' was all he could summon, in a whisper. He looked at her lovingly. She was dry, her yellow skin stretched tightly over her bones, her eyes were closed but it looked as if there were only sockets now where her eyes had once been. 'You were so beautiful.' he thought. Her dry hair was strewn across the bedsheet.

Ever so gently he touched her face. 'I love you,' was all that he had left to say to her. He carefully covered her body once more, and left the room to go and help the boys find Stephanie, Briony, Rachel and Veronica.

Derek prayed quietly to himself, he desperately hoped that they were unharmed. Maybe they escaped? Derek knew that the patron was an old lady, but she was nowhere to be seen either. He was sure that there was no way that she could have done this to Deirdre, for this was a monstrous, brutal, and terrifying attack. Perhaps she had escaped with the girls, or maybe they were hiding in the house, or the grounds?

He found the boys quickly, they were now up to the top floor, and they were searching for it methodically. Basically, it was one huge master suite up there in the eaves of the house. It had a huge bedroom with sofas, and a table and chairs for private dining. The ensuite had a large copper bath, and there was a separate dressing room almost as big again as the main bedroom.

'Any luck here?' he asked them. They answered, but he did not hear, his mind was still downstairs in Deirdre's bedroom.

'Nothing so far,' repeated Rich. Derek focused and noticed that every drawer, cupboard and wardrobe was open, things were strewn around, the covers pulled back on the bed, which was mercifully empty. There was nobody to be seen. They all called the girls names out again one by one, and then paused, waiting for a reply. The clock on the stairs struck 9am, and that was the only reply that they got.

'They must have got out somehow,' said Baz. 'Let's go see if there are outbuildings, maybe they are hiding in one of those.'

'OK, that makes sense,' said Derek.

They went downstairs to the entrance hall, and had another quick look around before going outside.

'If we find nothing outside, then there is no option but to for me to go and get help straight away,' said Derek. 'Maybe a search party can locate them. You boys must stay here near to the girls upstairs and ..Miss Rhymer. I will take the other lads with me. I don't like leaving you, but we can't leave them all..alone.'

'Good, good, that's it, leave them here, I will look after them now,' whispered Margaret's body from the secret basement. He had heard every word through the floorboards above him. 'Excellent, go now you foolish man, and when you return all here will be gone. Oh, such trouble you will be in,' The Hutenghast thought. It was convenient to stay as Margaret's body for now, soon he would have to reveal himself to them, and her form was more palatable than his own. This was now a game to him, rather than the last resort. It felt more like a blood sport.

Glancing at the girls laying there beside him he whispered, 'Soon you will be seven, soon, be patient my dears,' he laughed quietly to himself, and waited for the boys to return.

'I just get the feeling that they are still over there in the house somewhere,' said Colin, as they searched the grounds in vain. There were no outbuildings of any kind, which was odd for a substantial house such as this, but everything was odd about this place.

'When we go back inside, and Sir has gone to get help, we will look again, OK? There must be some hiding place in the house, maybe an attic space or a secret basement. Whatever it takes, we keep looking. We can't just sit here doing nothing, it's unbearable.'

'Agreed,' said Baz and Rich. They wanted to find the girls as desperately as any mother or father would.

'Poor Miss,' said Rich, he had clearly been thinking about her. 'What the hell happened?'

'It's that Hutenghast isn't it Col?' said Baz.

'Yes I think it is,' Colin said. 'But we'll find it, my gut feeling tells me the girls are alive, I think he needed them, or he needs them, and us too. That is what I got from the dreams; I think.'

'The sensible thing then would be to scarper, right?' said Rich.

'In theory yes, we could be at great risk ourselves staying here,' said Baz.

'In that case I say we arm ourselves and go back in,' said Rich. 'We are not leaving without BB and the others.'

'That's right, we stay here together, or we leave together,' said Colin. They both nodded.

'OK boys, we have exhausted this search, we need more help,' said Derek as he came back over. 'As discussed you stay here, but if you hear anything, then go and hide in the woods. I will be back as quickly as I can.' He smiled weakly, and jogged away towards the statue.

'Get whatever you can find as a weapon, we will go back in armed like Rich says,' Colin said in a determined way. 'That thing has got them, and we are going to get 'it'. Come on let's go.'

They went back into the house armed with just sticks and stones, and a bravery beyond the bravest of men.

Chapter 46

Derek got back to the statue quickly. 'Where are the others?' the boys exclaimed.

'Waiting at the house. Where are Henderson and those Duke twins?' said Derek, quickly diverting the conversation away from the obvious, that being that he was now alone.

'They went in the same direction as you,' one of the boys said. 'It looked to us like they were following you, we didn't ask questions.'

'Bloody hell!' said Derek. 'Well, they will have to fend for themselves until we get back that's all. Come on, we have to go back down the mountain to get help. There has been an incident, no questions now please, time is of the essence, let's go. Oh, by the way did anyone get a mobile signal?'

'No, sorry,' came the reply. They all started back down the track.

In the woods nearby Keith Henderson and the Dukes came out of hiding. 'We need to go back to the house. You saw those three picking up sticks and stones before going back inside. Something bad has happened, it's obvious. None of the girls have come out have they? Nor has Miss for that matter. Sir wouldn't leave them, or us, unless it was an emergency, so let's go,' said Keith.

'This is ace,' said Peter Duke.

'What do you mean by that,' said Keith.

'The most fun we have had on this lousy trip so far, right bro?' he said to his brother Brian.

'You said it,' he replied. 'Perhaps they have all been murdered, how cool would that be?'

'I can't believe you two,' said Keith. 'What the hell is wrong with you, you idiots? They could all really be in danger.'

'Yes, but it is not our problem, is it bro,' Brian pointed out, and Peter agreed.

'You morons, it is <u>all</u> our problem. We are all here together. I'm going back, are you coming, or not?' Keith spat the words out

'Listen you,' said Brian giving him a shove. 'Pete and me just look out for us, right. You wanna go get sweet Rachel, then you go alone. We are just going down the hill to watch old Fordy get arrested by the police. That should be a laugh.' His brother laughed loudly in response. 'Yeah he's in trouble up to his neck.'

Keith looked at them incredulously. These two boys that he had kept company with over the last few years were showing their true colours. He always knew that they were bad, but they really did not care about anybody, even now in a situation as dire as this, that appeared to be deteriorating even further before their very eyes. They could not see it, there was no empathy, not a trace of concern. The scales were well and truly removed from Keith's eyes in that moment, and he realised that he was now truly and utterly alone. The Dukes were leaving, Colin, Baz and Rich hated him, and so did everyone else, and who could blame them? He had been so self-absorbed ever since his mum had died. He had lost sight of what was truly important. Those three, and the girls had it right. Friends, true friends, that was what mattered.

Something bad had happened up at the house, the girls were missing, Mr Ford had left them behind, and even though they could be in desperate danger, Colin, Barry and Richard had gone back into the house anyway, armed with only sticks and stones. Time to go.

He turned and ran back towards the house without another word to the Dukes. He heard them say 'loser' to his back, but he didn't care, they were the losers here, and he was done with them, for good.

'Whatever happens now, is going to happen,' he thought. His mind went to his mum too, she was always so kind and considerate to everyone. It made him feel guilty about his own behaviour. 'What would she do in this situation,' thought Keith. She would go and help, he knew that.

As he approached the house he saw what looked like an old iron railing spike on the grass. He tried to pick it up, but it was buried deep, and stuck fast, so he grabbed a few stones like the others had done. He put them into his pockets, and he jogged back to the house. He was going to help.

Inside, Colin and the others had started searching for a second time. They had decided to do it quietly, no calling of names. Nobody was going to answer that was for certain. Colin went upstairs to the bedroom to check that everything was still as it had been left by them. The girls were there, still out of it, but OK. The bed was untouched, Miss was still in there, he didn't look. Being a smart lad, he knew not to tamper. This was a crime scene now, a murder scene! The Hutenghast had done this, there was no other explanation. Nobody could explain this to the police, they would think that they were all mad, or worse still complicit in some way.

As he walked back down the stairs, he saw the others coming out of the library. 'This Hutenghast, he's done all this. He's killed Miss, he's got the girls, and we're going to get him,' he said.

The others felt the same way, they were all scared, their hands were shaking, and their knees felt weak. They felt sick too, but the fury that came from the knowledge that some malevolent thing had done this to their friends, and killed their teacher to boot, gave them a steely resolve. They were going to get this Hutenghast thing, or die in the attempt.

Margaret's body heard the voice above. They were back, and they were alone. He could sense that, just the last three, Time to get this done.

He moved silently to the basement stairs, it was dark down there, just one small transom window letting any light in, but that did not matter, even in the old woman's body he could still see like an animal. He climbed the stairs up to the secret door. He pushed a lever on the wall beside it, and a panel in the entrance hall opened. He walked through, and it closed behind him.

The boys were now in the kitchen, he could hear them opening the cupboard doors. This was it. Margaret's body moved silently across the space between, and entered the kitchen.

Keith was at the house now. He was looking through the kitchen window from outside. He saw the boys searching, all the cabinet doors were open in the kitchen, and the larder door was ajar. Rich was inside the larder pulling out large boxes on the floor, and looking inside. He was just about to tap the window, and then he thought, they don't actually want me here. They hate me. I will just follow and watch, for now.

He was just about to walk round to the front door, when he saw an old woman come into the kitchen. 'That must be the owner,' he thought. She just stood there watching the three friends, why didn't she say something? She was shielded from Richard's view, but if the others had looked, they would have seen her. Keith looked at her face, something was off here, what was it? She was smiling, but it was not a kind smile, it made his flesh crawl. Then she stopped and raised her head a little. It looked like she was sniffing the air like a dog would do. Then her head snapped round towards him. He felt that she had sensed that he was watching. He ducked out of sight, just in time.

'There is nothing in here,' said Rich coming back into the main kitchen.

Now they were all together, Margaret's body could get to work. Closing the kitchen door silently The Hutenghast spoke to them for the first time.

'Looking for anything in particular?' he said.

Keith was looking through the window again. He could hear the old woman's voice, although it was muffled by the glass. It didn't sound like an old woman's voice at all. It was deep, and sort of menacing. He didn't like the look or the sound of this woman. Wherever the girls were, she was behind this. He wanted to run to the front so that he could come and assist. There was no rear kitchen door, he had already walked around the perimeter. There was only one door and that was the main front door. He hesitated, he wanted to watch and listen here before he did anything else.

All the boy's turned towards the voice. They could see it was probably the old woman that owned the place.

'Where are the girls?' said Colin.

'Do not worry my dear, they are safe, they are hidden. Would you like to see them?' The voice was absolutely mesmerising to them, it wrapped itself around them like a snake. They had a strong urge to just comply, it was like their freewill was being drained away.

Barry shook his head and briefly came to his senses. 'Where is The Hutenghast?' he said.

The old woman looked surprised. 'They know my name; how can that be?' he thought. 'The woman Margaret had not seen them; it makes no sense.' Then he realised, 'It was the boy's father.' He was impressed but he did not show it. He spoke for a second time.

'Ah the beast, yes he came and killed the woman, the girl children all fainted, but I managed to get four of them away safely. He may come back at any time. I am scared of him; we must all hide together.'

None of this rang true, this voice was not that of an old woman. It was not of this world. Colin realised this.

'Show yourself,' was all he said. 'Come on, show yourself. My Dad is not afraid of you, and nor am I. We want the girls, where are they?' His glare was strong as he looked into the old woman's eyes, but so dark were they, and menacing too, with the light flickering red around the edges, that he could not hold the gaze for long.

'You are clever boy,' said Margaret's body. 'The time for pretence is over. Yes I have them, and now I have you. How glorious this is.'

'Are they near, are they like the others upstairs?' said Barry

'They sleep yes, they are waiting. Waiting for you.'

The boys held their sticks in front of them, and moved forward. Margaret's body laughed; this was sport indeed.

'You have come armed I see,' he said. 'But I don't think I will surrender. It is you who will surrender. Seven I need, and seven I have. All were chosen, all are here. Now come, all will be well.'

Margaret's body went to sweep their consciousness away, but hesitated a moment as the boy Richard spoke.

'OK, this seven business. What is it? We want to know. We realise who you are. We can't stop you, we know that too, so just tell us. Or are you too scared to?'

It was a brave and reckless thing to do thought Keith as he looked on from his vantage point, which was now in the hallway.

The Hutenghast was arrogant and overconfident (the Great Being knew this).

'Very well,' he said. 'You can be told.'

He waved an arm and said words that Keith did not understand, but clearly it had an effect. The boys were still awake, they stood, but they could no longer move.

'A captive audience,' laughed the old woman.

'You seven are here at my bidding, I need your…assistance. It is required for me to…'

'Live?' interrupted Colin.

'Clever boy, I knew your father once. But he is dead now.'

'You liar!' shouted Colin.

'Maybe, maybe not, but you will never know boy. That woman upstairs, the instructor.'

'Teacher,' corrected Barry.

This correction was ignored.

'That is your fate boy, all the seven are needed. I am here to take you to myself.'

Although the boys were immobile, they could still move their eyes as well as their mouths. Colin looked around. That was when he spotted Keith Henderson in the hall, their eyes met, and he knew that potentially all was not lost.

'Look we are helpless, we can't move. You are going to kill us, we know that, but we want to see the girls first,' said Colin. He did not know where this strength came from exactly, despite the odds here, he was so calm, he felt like the eye of a storm. He reasoned that this Hutenghast would tell them anything now. No point in hiding anymore when you have already won.

'OK, so you will kill us like you did Miss but why, and why seven?'

Margaret's body spoke,
'Always was it so
Heavens above
And Earth below
Seven souls I need to take
Replenishment for me they make
I live to live
You live to die
Twas always thus
Don't ask me why'

'But I do ask,' said Colin 'As we have no hope here, tell me how we could have beaten you. Nothing is infallible right? Even someone as awesome as you. What could we have done?'

The Hutenghast was arrogant, but he was not stupid. There was no need to say anything more now, he could just do what needed to be done. But the thought of telling them everything, and then they would go to their deaths knowing that they could have stopped him so easily, but had failed so miserably, was just too delicious to resist.

Margaret's body laughed. And then stood upright and still. The boys (including the silent Keith), looked on, waiting to see what the old woman would say or do next. As they watched, cracks started to appear on her skin, like a crackle glazed pot. The cracks grew bigger, and then they burst as if there had been an explosion. Dust filled the air momentarily, and then as it cleared, they saw the beast as he truly was. The Hutenghast had come!

Keith stifled a scream, but the others were less surprised. 'So, this was the enemy,' he thought.

As anger overruled all their fears Rich said, 'Come on then spill the beans, we are all getting bored here.'

The Hutenghast laughed.

'Well, boy children, neither you nor the girl children have read or heard 'The Telling' spoken so I cannot take you as I did the woman. She read this.'

A parchment tied in a black ribbon appeared in his left hand. And then he drew a knife from his torso with his right. 'Behold the Knife Of Life And Death.'

He paused and they all looked at the knife, the handle was made of what looked like bone, and the blade was long and thin, it had a blue tinge to it.

He continued: -
'The Hutenghast can only come
 For those who hear this from a tongue' (He held aloft the parchment).
 'I cannot speak these words through
 It will not work from me to you
 The Telling is a call to me,

But spoken not by me
Can't you see?
For my will this work is done
I cannot rest till everyone
Who has heard The Telling spoken freely
Sleeps before they come to me'

'Ha, Ha, Ha.'
'Since you are all about to die, there is one more thing I will tell you. The secret.

Before I kill you whether seven or one
Before you close your eyes and come
If you have only seen 'The Telling'
Not read aloud, and you are willing
You have the power, though it sounds absurd
To take me down, you have my word
You may end my reign, my glory
Do me down, finish my story.
For if you hold this parchment thus'

They all watched as The Hutenghast held the parchment over his breast where his heart should be beating (although they doubted that he had a heart).
'Then take this Knife Of Life And Death,
And thrust it through the Telling
Saying 'Hutenghast be gone!'
The spell will break for everyone
Whoever has been called to me
If their body remains they will be freed
Their moisture and their soul regain
From dust to life be born again'

He laughed, 'Simple, is it not? A piece of paper and a knife was all you needed to save your life.'

Out of the shadows Keith jumped, and he ran at great speed, as if possessed, towards The Hutenghast. Too late, his presence was felt. The beast realised that this was the boy from earlier that had been dismissed from his thoughts. Now he realised in horror, that it was to his own detriment. For before he could react the knife was already out of his hand, and Keith had it. He plunged it through the parchment that was still held to The Hutenghast's breast, and said the words 'Hutenghast be gone.' The knife was sharp, and it was cold, so cold.

A cloud of moisture started to leave the Hutenghast, it swirled above his head and then went out of the door, straight up the stairs and into the bedroom above where it re-entered Deirdre's inert and lifeless body. The parchment became like ash and disappeared. The knife began to melt, it was now a bright red. It dripped on the floor like a candle's wax, and then it was gone. The Hutenghast's face jerked, and writhed, and twitched. No words came out of his mouth, for he had spoken his last. His eyes flickered and became as dead. Then cracks appeared all over his skin, as they had done on the old woman's body, but this time he simply exploded into dust, and was no more.

Immediately, the boys could move again. Colin grabbed Keith's shaking hand, which was still clutching the bone handle of the knife. He let it slip to the floor.

'Come on Keith,' he said, 'Let's all go and find where that thing has hidden the girls.'

Chapter 47

Derek and the rest of the boys went back down the mountain track as fast as they could safely go. He spoke little, and all the boys could see from the tight expression on his face, and his short demeanour, that something was very wrong, and they were all concerned, and somewhat afraid. Derek heard mumblings of 'telling parents' this and that, and 'wish we had never come on this trip'. He felt like screaming, 'I wish I hadn't come on this bloody trip either!' But of course, he did not say that.

He knew his career was over, and his life was ruined. As he walked he had thought that the authorities may hold him responsible in some way. He was scared about that, Deirdre was dead, he had abandoned her and the girls. Some of the girls were in some kind of trance or coma, and the rest were nowhere to be seen. The perfect nightmare for a teacher in charge of a school trip. They were going to throw the book at him, and who could blame them? Derek couldn't! But there was no time to feel sorry about his own predicament, his main concern now had to be getting the children back home to their families. This was a recon. exercise now, the trip was done, and so was he.

As they approached the fork that led to the village, Derek heard loud footsteps coming up behind them. He turned around to see Peter and Brian Duke coming towards them. The party waited for them to catch up, and Derek said, 'Where have you two been and where is Henderson?'

'We were scared, we didn't know what to do,' they lied. 'After you abandoned us all, and let the others stay up there all alone after the girls didn't come out. We figured something was wrong Sir, but Keith was so horrible to us, and told us to clear off. He wanted to stay there on his own, and watch the fun. At least that is what he said, whatever that all means Sir,' continued Brian Duke.

Derek may have been in a state of shock, and not necessarily thinking too clearly, but one thing was certainly true, and that was that practically every utterance that Peter and Brian Duke ever made was a lie. They were bad news. He decided to take this as just another lie. 'OK you two, come with us now. I will see to all this when we come back.'

Both the Dukes had a smug look on their faces, Derek could have belted them round the ear right there and then for playing games and telling lies at a time like this, but for now there were more important things to worry about, and he didn't want to add assault and battery to his long list of failings.

Derek was just considering whether to carry on down to the lake or stop at the village first, when the bartender Fritz came bounding down the track towards them. He had a concerned look on his face.

'The main phone line is up now, but no mobile service yet,' he said 'I have contacted the café at the lake below, and they are sending up some people to help. Hermann, sees everything, he is always in the woods. He told me that you are separated still. There is a problem, yes? We wish to help.'

'Yes, there is a problem,' said a deflated Derek. 'Some of the girls are missing. The others appear to be in a deep sleep, maybe drugged, I don't know. Deirdre, er the other teacher, Miss Rhymer is.. um indisposed, she cannot help. I have left some of the boys up there to keep a watch over them all. We need to find help quickly.'

Fritz could see that Derek was very close to breaking point. 'They are all on their way to help. Come my friend, we will go back to the house together now, and I will assist you in finding the girls, yes? They will be OK, I know this,' he said rather unconvincingly.

Derek's brain had pretty much reached full capacity, it was all too much to take in. He simply followed Fritz like a little sheep now, as they all retraced their steps back up to the house that they had only left a mere forty minutes before. The boys were very subdued, apart from the Duke twins that is, who were lapping up all this drama like a cat at the cream.

As Derek and Co. were retracing their steps, back at the house the four boys had left the kitchen, and were back in the entrance hall.

'Well that certainly did it,' said Baz at last.

'Boy when you came running in Keith, and you grabbed that knife. Well that took guts man. You saved our lives,' said Rich. He extended his hand and Keith took it.

'I couldn't do anything else could I? I mean, I'm sorry for, well everything, you know, how I have been and..'

Colin cut in, 'You will never have to explain a single thing to us mate. You are one of us now. Let's find the girls.'

'SHH,' said Baz, and they all stood still, and listened. The only sound that could be heard was that wretched clock on the stairs, but then Rich said, 'Did you hear that?' he pointed to the wall. 'I heard a noise, there, behind there. Like a thump.'

They all listened, and they all definitely heard it the second time. They went over to where the noise came from, and started tapping the wall. There was a part of it that sounded hollow.

Then they heard voices upstairs.

'You two go upstairs and see if the girls are waking up. Don't touch the bed!' Colin said to Baz and Keith. 'Rich and I will try to get this open, there must be a latch or a lever somewhere.'

'This is definitely a false panel,' said Rich. He banged the wall twice, and they both listened. After a few moments the reply came, thud, thud. 'That must be the girls,' said Colin. 'That Hutenghast thing must have had them all in a spell or something, and now he's gone, they are all waking up.

'CAN YOU HEAR ME?' shouted Colin at the top of his lungs.

'Yes,' came a muffled reply. It was Steph.

Colin's heart leapt with joy.

'STEPH, THERE MUST BE A LEVER THERE OR SOMETHING THAT OPENS UP THIS PANEL, CAN YOU SEE IT?' he shouted.

Upstairs the boys were just about to go in the bedroom when Baz stopped Keith with his arm. 'Look mate,' he said, 'The thing is, Miss, she is..'

He didn't get to finish as the girls all came out, and greeted them on the landing.

'Where is Miss?' said Keith.

'Here I am,' said Deirdre, as she came out of the door, she looked awful, pale and lifeless, but amazingly she wasn't dead, she was very much alive.

'I had the worst dream ever, last night. I thought I was..'
'Dead?' said Keith.
'How did you know?'
'Oh, just a wild guess,' he replied.
'But you were dead Miss!' the girls started to say, but Baz stopped them.
'No, she was just a bit more out of it than you all were, that's all. Come on Rich and Colin are downstairs looking for the others,' he said quickly changing the subject. 'You wait here Miss; we will be back in a jiffy.'

Without a word, and with a puzzled look on her face she turned around and went back into the bedroom, and sat on the bed.

Downstairs, the two boys were looking around, they were tapping and pulling anything on the wall, pictures, a barometer, a taxidermy head of a wild boar.

On the other side Steph, BB, Rach and V were all wide awake, the surroundings could not really be seen properly, as they were mostly in darkness.

'What happened to us exactly?' said V.
'I'm not quite sure,' said Steph. 'I went to find Miss, and the old lady was there by her door. I wanted to go in, but she wouldn't let me. Then I think Miss was in bed, I think she was..'
'Dead,' said BB.
'Yes, YES!' Steph replied. 'That Margaret was there, but it wasn't her, I know it. It was some creature and then..blank, I can't remember anything else. We have to get out of here. Wherever here is.'

'I think it is the cellar or basement of the house, but I don't know how we got here,' said Rach.

'It must have been that thing that brought us down here,' said BB shaking at the mere thought of it. 'What was that thing?'

Colin's Dad's nightmare, that's what,' said Steph.

'Well, it is not here now, so let's go find the others and then go find Sir, and the boys,' said V.

'Yes, I think...wait a minute did you hear that voice?' said Rach.

'It was Colin!' squealed Steph. 'He asked if we could hear him. YES, WE CAN,' she shouted in response.

They followed the sound in the semi darkness, and climbed some wooden steps that led to a wall, there was no door to be seen (or felt) at all.

'I think he said look for a switch or something, so feel around, and pull or twist anything you touch,' said Rach.

'Uck, if I feel anything, I will tell you about it, and you can do that pulling and twiddling thing,' said V.

'Come on girls, let's just get out of here, OK?' said Steph.

Without another word they started fumbling around, pulling and twisting anything that came to hand. At last, a click was heard, and the wall moved a fraction, just sufficient to allow the light to trickle in.

The boys had also seen this movement in the wall on the other side, and they yanked it open just at precisely the same time as Derek and the boys came through the front door with Fritz in tow. The rest of the girls were coming down the stairs with Keith and Baz behind them too, and unbelievably they were followed by a dazed and very disoriented Deirdre, who had come to her senses sufficiently enough to recall where they all were, and what was happening here.

What actually happened next was a little like a farcical comedy sketch. They all clapped eyes on each other at precisely the same time. The rush of excitement and relief overcame everyone instantly. All reserve and any self-conscious thoughts or embarrassment from open signs of affection were simply swept aside as they all rushed into each other's arms. The girls ran down the stairs followed by Baz and Keith, the boys ran into the house to greet them, all apart from the Duke twins that is, whose reverie at this mayhem now quickly turned to dismay, as they realised that it was them that were probably going to be in trouble here now, once again.

Fritz stood back and watched the melee with a satisfied smile on his face (Hermann had appeared beside him from nowhere and he looked equally pleased).

Derek felt a wave of relief as the children all greeted each other excitedly, chattering away like chipmunks. He had completely forgotten the weight of his troubles momentarily at the sheer euphoria on view here. Then he saw Deirdre stood on the stair next to the all-seeing clock. His knees went weak, and he thought he was going to pass out as the blood drained from his face. A millisecond later, and after a double take, he knew that his eyes did not deceive him. Not thinking of what the children may think about any of this, he sprinted across the hallway, and bounded up the stairs two at a time. He half expected Deirdre to vanish in a puff of smoke as he wrapped his arms around her, but she did not, this was real. He held her close, she felt cold like she had been outside in winter without a coat or gloves. He drew back and gazed into her eyes, she looked very tired, but apart from being a little pallid, she was as beautiful a sight as he had ever seen. He kissed her on the lips, smelled her hair, it really was..real. Stupidly he said, 'Is it really you?'

Deirdre was weak, but from the moment she had seen Derek coming up the stairs towards her, her heart had begun to beat faster, pumping the blood around her body, re-oxygenating the limbs and organs that made her what she was, a veritable walking miracle.

'But, you were, I mean I thought that,' stumbled Derek.

'I was dead?'

'Yes, I mean that is what it looked like.'

'Well apparently I was, but now I'm not. So, go figure,' she said, her humour clearly returning. 'Boy does that brandy pack a punch!'

'What brandy?' said Derek perplexed.

'Oh nothing, just babbling,' replied Deirdre.

'Well, Deirdre Rhymer, this is without doubt the best day of my life,' he continued. 'I thought that I had lost you, I was so..'

'Scared?'

'I was going to say bereft, but yes that too. I don't understand any of what has happened here, and I don't really care to either. The authorities are coming and there will be explaining to do, but whatever happens, I will take full responsibility. I left you, I will never forgive myself for doing that.'

'It was my fault as much as yours, we were both stubborn and stupid. We are in this together. I think the main problem now will be explaining about the old woman, Margaret.'

'Yes where is she?'

'Gone, like I was I suppose. I don't really know, but I don't think that she will be coming back.'

Derek held her close again, and they kissed once more. Not a single child even witnessed this shocking display, they were far too busy with their own reunions.

Whilst all this was happening, Baz and Keith had made their way across the hallway to the open wall panel. They stood there alongside Colin and Rich as Steph, BB, Rach and V stepped back into the daylight. Just like everyone else in that joyous moment, in that creepy house that was all alone up on a mountainside. A house that had been the scene of things darker than anybody should have to witness or endure, these two particular quartets, the seven plus one (their saviour), just stood there for a second or two, drinking in the sight of each other, and then the rest of the room, and finally they all looked specifically at the person that meant the most to them at that particular moment.

Colin and Steph had been friends forever, and that was, and always had been OK, but Steph had gotten to think of Colin as a little staid, safe, unexciting, this last year or so. Rich seemed so carefree, more fun, and so their relationship had dipped a little recently. They had confided in each other less and less, they spent time alone together rarely, in short they had drifted apart. Steph had not been too concerned about this at the time, although she could tell that Colin was a little irked at her fascination with Rich, but that was OK, they were just friends after all. But this trip had galvanised her thoughts, she now felt differently, the dynamic had changed for her. She had worried a lot about Colin and his dad these last couple of days, and when she saw that he was anguished, and when things started to get rough. Like the fog, and Miss being in that state (which she realised was now in the past as she saw her in an embrace with Derek on the stair). The only person that she had thought of, wanted to be with, and hold his hand and take comfort in his presence, was Colin. Good old Colin, reliable old Colin. He was her rock, and she was his. They looked unblinking into each other's eyes. Colin spoke first (he stammered a little for the first time that whole trip) 'I, I was so so worried. We thought that you might be, be.'

'No, you can't get rid of us that easily,' said Steph. 'We missed you, that is to say, I er..missed you.'

'Me too,' said Colin and they embraced. Both of them felt that feeling in the pit of their stomachs, but being only twelve years old, they just took it to mean excitement and relief, but it was more than that, it was love.

BB looked at Rich who flushed. 'You took your time,' she said.

'I'm sorry, we got here as quickly as we could, I was looking for you, we were looking for all of you. Then we had to contend with..'

'Yes I know about him,' BB cut in. 'I was scared, we all were, but I knew that you would come for us, and that everything would be OK.'

'Yep, you would never have let me live it down if I hadn't come first thing this morning. Truth is nothing could have stopped us. We were on a mission, Colin's mission I guess, but for me it was all mostly about…you,' he gulped.

BB's eyes welled up, she hugged him hard and whispered in his ear, 'I missed you so much Richard Jenkins, I'm so glad you are here with me now when I needed you.'

Baz and V were less formal. She just grabbed him and gave him another one of her big kisses. 'I like these,' he thought as he was being crushed. 'You are quite a wonder, all of you, we are the magnificent seven right?' said V.

'Well actually we have a new member,' said Baz stepping away, and putting his arm around Keith's shoulder. 'I don't know if any of you recall who this guy is but.'

'He saved us all!' cut in Rich. 'Keith Henderson is our hero, he slayed the beast.'

'Seven became eight,' said Colin.

'Well as you all know, I do like prime numbers, but even numbers are more, balanced,' said BB.

Keith appeared a little awkward, his eyes were looking down at his shoes. Rach stepped forward. 'Thank you Keith,' she said 'I always knew that you were..'

'A good egg?' said V.

They all laughed. 'Yes I suppose so, but more than that.'

'He's your good egg?' said Rich.

They all laughed again, and Rach took Keith's hands in her own, and looked at him for several moments. His eyes left his shoes, and he returned her gaze. 'I would have died trying to get to you,' he said earnestly.

'I know that, you know I knew that, don't you,' she replied.
'Yes.'

They hugged. It was the first time Keith that had been held in a loving way since his mum's funeral. Any ice that was still running through his veins melted right there and then as they embraced. Tears welled up in his eyes, and he did not try to hide them, he was done with hiding.

After a minute or two everyone had regained their composure. Questions were asked and answered. They had come to the conclusion that The Hutenghast had been some kind of demon, an intruder that invaded your dreams. It had killed Miss, but the spell had been broken, and she had returned. Also, it had visited Colin's dad for some reason that was not clear. Maybe just to be 'bad'. Whatever the reason was, it had been enough for him to be able to warn Colin in some telekinetic way. It had been enough, they were all alive, even Miss who was miraculously still here. The story of the Telling, and the means to end The Hutenghast once and for all, was relayed as each person's recollections were taken into account. Keith's heroic entrance was heard with gasps and pats on the back accompanied by 'Well done,' and 'Thank you.' It felt good to him, he belonged again. Only the Duke twins still looked miserable.

'This is all lovely,' said Brian Duke, 'But what about the old lady. The police will want to know what happened to her won't they,' he looked at Derek as he said this.

'There is no old woman,' an unfamiliar voice said.

They all looked around and noticed that Fritz and Hermann were still there, looking on.

'What was that?' said Derek.

'I said there is no old woman,' replied Hermann, in a sort of trance like state. 'I live in these woods, I watch, I see everything. This Hutenghast, I have seen him, both awake and asleep. He is gone now, but evil he was. The old woman, she was once real, but he tricked her, she sold her soul to him many years ago. She had become like a picture on a screen, there to see, but no longer real. The Hutenghast needed souls to survive, seven young souls. The old woman was an apparition, and his servant. It was she that tricked you all into coming here. You were to be consumed much like the lady,' he looked at Deirdre and smiled. 'But nothing is certain, life is never clear, every now and then a little fog is good. The old lady failed, the fog came, it changed the landscape. The Hutenghast needed to act quickly to survive, he took the old woman to himself, and she became dust. Dust like she should have become so long ago. You boys, you clever boys made the beast reveal his one and only weakness, his Achilles heel. You dispatched him. He is not of this earth, and therefore there is no crime here. There are no bodies, there is no evidence. You may leave here in peace.' The Great Being finished speaking through Hermann, who had been his eyes and ears all this time.

'Blimey,' said Colin after a few moments. 'How did you know all this, I mean how exactly do you know this stuff.'

'Evil has its servants, just as good has its followers. There is a balance that needs to be maintained. For every Hutenghast there is a..'

'God?' Deirdre said cutting in.

'I prefer to say a Greater Being,' said Hermann. 'There will be no inquiry, nobody will come to ask questions of you. You may leave anytime. This place is empty now, it is no longer needed, the trees and nature will take it to their bosom. Your ordeal is at an end. You seven.'

The Great Being left Hermann and he looked at the crowd again but this time with his own eyes. 'I, that is Fritz, and I will escort you down to the lake now. It will be our privilege to do so.'

Fritz looked at Hermann. Those few souls that lived here in the hamlet, the small village were so close to this place. They were aware of the darkness that dwelled about the place. Fritz had always had a feeling that Hermann knew more than the rest of them. He was a God-fearing man, as they all were. He knew that there had been an intervention here. It was a good intervention, and that was enough for Fritz, he did not question Hermann, their task now was to take these good people back down the mountain to be re-united with their loved ones.

Nobody questioned any of this logic, why would you? They had been in the most dangerous and precarious situation. It was so strange because things had happened, creatures had been seen that were not of this world. Their lives had all been in peril, they should have been afraid, damaged, broken. But they were not, there was a euphoria, it felt like the first day of Spring. Their lives were in sharp focus like never before. What had passed was now gone, and the future was as bright as any future could possibly be, and they revelled in it as they walked back down the mountain. Even the Duke twins were happy, they were off the hook, and that was a small win for them. Keith looked at them as he walked hand in hand with Rachel, he pitied them, and he was glad that he was no longer one of them. His own personal fog had been lifted from his eyes, and he was truly happy for the first time since that holiday abroad with his mum and dad.

Chapter 48

The headmaster and his secretary had made all the necessary phone calls. It had been a difficult morning. Mrs Hart had been a great help, and within a few hours all the parents and the headmaster himself were on a flight to Munich International Airport. Everything had been arranged, the coach driver from Watts Coaches would meet them at the airport, and take them on to Lake Eibsee. Apparently a man had turned up at the driver's sister's house in Stuttgart only that morning. Super Mario had opened the door to him. The man had thrust a map into his hand. It was an ordnance survey map of the surrounding area. There was a red biro line on it which seemed to trace a path from Lake Eibsee up a nearby mountain. 'You must go there, now. The children there are in need of you,' the man had said. Before he could question him about this, the man was gone. Super Mario had turned his head to speak to his sister who was stood behind him at the door, and when he looked back the man had simply vanished into thin air.

The coach company had called him earlier, and asked him many questions. He knew that something maybe had gone wrong. Without hesitation he made a call. The coach was waiting for them as they exited the Arrivals Lounge.

'This way, everybodies,' he said holding up a placard with the school's name on it. Nobody asked questions, they did not want to waste any time. Within minutes they were on the coach as it sped on to its destination. It was a miracle but there next to Mrs Hart sat her husband. His recovery had been miraculous, he was still weak and thin, but the hospital could not deny that he was fit enough to travel. He would have to come back for further tests of course upon his return, but they reasoned now that he had suffered enough. Holding him there would just take more of a toll on him, and so they released him.

All the other parents were there too, Keith's father, Mrs Duke, all the gang's parents. Everyone who could possibly be there was present. They chatted amongst themselves very little on that short trip. The headmaster felt much as Derek had done. He felt totally responsible, and totally guilty too. It weighed heavily on him as he sat there. He was brought out of this melancholy by the feel of a hand on his shoulder. It was Mr Hart.

''Don't worry, there was nothing you could do, I know how it feels to be helpless, but there is help for the helpless. The children are fine. I know this is true. Please don't beat yourself up. This is going to be a good day.'

The headmaster looked into Mr Hart's earnest eyes. he could tell that he had suffered greatly these last six months. He felt bad for worrying more about his own position here, it felt shallow to do that.

'I am so glad you are here Mr Hart,' he said. 'I hope you are right.'

'The beast is gone,' said Mr Hart as he sat back down in the seat behind him next to his wife. It was the same seats that Colin and Rich had sat in only a couple of days before.

The coach pulled in at the lake side, and they all got off. It had been decided that Mr Hart was too weak to go up the track. He would wait in the café with one other person from each family. Mostly the men were going ahead, and the women were waiting here, apart from Mrs Hart and Mrs Duke that is.

It was a beautiful day, and they sat at tables outside overlooking the lake. A few 'Goodbyes,' 'See you soons,' and 'Don't worrys,' were exchanged, and then the hikers set off across the car park and onto the track that the children had taken. Super Mario was in the lead with the map, and they all followed him. He had been expecting some epic trudge up the mountain, and so he had borrowed some walking boots from his brother-in-law (who was a similar size to him), to make the arduous trip easier. It was therefore a little bit of a disappointment to him when they had travelled little more than one hundred yards or so, and he spotted a party coming down the mountain towards them. His eyesight was good, very good. He realised immediately that it was them. 'There,' he said pointing. 'There they are. Here we come to find them, and they find us.'

Everybody squinted in the general direction. They could see figures, but nobody could really tell if it was them, or just another group of hikers. They were dots on the horizon, but they didn't care about that. Faith made them run.

'Look,' said Peter Duke to his brother, 'That's mum!' He had eyes like a hawk.

'It's all our parents,' said BB 'And the Headmaster too.'

'Oh no!' said Derek.

'Don't worry,' said Deirdre, who was holding his hand. 'It's all good.'

'Yes,' said Hermann, 'This is as it should be.' He touched Fritz on the arm, and they stopped walking just as the rest of the ensemble started to run down the track to meet their welcoming party.

'We have done what was needed to be done,' he said to Fritz, and they smiled at the sight of everyone running downhill with abandon. They turned and walked back to the village, unnoticed.

Rich could easily have got there quicker than everybody else as he was the fastest kid in school, but he stayed with BB. They exchanged beams of joy as they ran, as did the rest of the party. This was like a cork coming out of the champagne bottle with all the fizz behind it. The gap between the two parties diminished quickly enough, even though the parents had slowed to a walk. The kids and the teachers kept pace. This was so surreal, Derek looked at Deirdre as they ran. 'This is all really happening isn't it? I'm not having a dream, or a nightmare am I?' he said.

'No, this is no nightmare, this is heaven,' she replied.

They converged at speed, peeling away as they did so from each other to greet their loved ones. Colin went to his mum and hugged her, tears in his eyes. Baz and Rich, Steph, BB, V and Rach all embraced their fathers like they had just come back from a warzone. Keith saw his father, and he stopped. His father kept moving, he threw his arms around his son, and held him tight. 'Forgive me boy,' he said. Keith wept, his life was truly complete, his heart was healed in that moment.

The Dukes thought they were going to get a belt round the ear, but their mum hugged them. 'You two, trouble is never far behind you. Just like your father. He says hello by the way.' She kissed them both on the forehead, which was quite the sign of affection, they turned and walked down the path.

Derek and Deirdre stood in front of the headmaster. There was an awkward silence. 'I'm so sorry,' Derek and the headmaster said simultaneously. They looked puzzled as they were both expecting a grilling from the other. 'I am so sorry that I sent you on this mad trip,' said the headmaster. 'I am going to hand in my resignation.'

'Sir,' said Deirdre. 'Don't you dare, this has been the worst, and also the best experience of my life. I would never be feeling like this, if we had not all come here. I am so happy I could cry,' and she did.

'Sir, this has been an adventure I won't forget,' said Derek. 'It's not your fault here, you see there was a fog, and well we got separated and..'

Colin cut in 'What happened on the mountain, stays on the mountain. This was all supposed to be, we can't change anything, we just reacted to it. We stuck together, and we are all here, all safe, happy, and wiser. Can we just be content with that?'

'You will do well at your new school Colin,' said the headmaster as he placed a hand on the boy's shoulder. 'Time to come and see your Dad at the café over there I think. What do you say?'

Colin was speechless, he just ran.

Well, reunions are the sweetest of things. Even Super Mario got hugs from children, parents and even a certain teacher who had diced with death.

As they all laughed, and drank wine, and cordial, and lemonade in that café by the lake on that beautiful afternoon, the gang of eight stood there together looking across the water, as the light danced across its surface.

'Doesn't get any better than this does it?' said Colin.

'Nope,' said Steph.

The boys looked at each other, and smiled, and the girls did the same. They all linked arms.

'We are all friends for life now, right?' said Keith.

'Yep, you are one of us now, like it or not,' said Rach.

'I like it, I like it a lot, said Keith.

There were many important things in the universe that were of concern to the Great Being at that moment on that day, but none more so than this. One darkness had been extinguished here, but he knew that evil was still out there, just waiting to reappear like a forest fire. He had to be ever watchful, he could never be complacent. That had been his task since the beginning of everything. And as he looked down on those few happy souls' below in their moment of reunion. He was truly, truly content.

THE END

The story continues in

'The Bone Handle'

Coming November 2023

Milton Keynes UK
Ingram Content Group UK Ltd.
UKHW020628140823
426838UK00016B/811